Forgiven

MAY 2010

CH

Forgiven

Forgiven

Vanessa Miller

www.urbanchristianonline.net

Urban Books, LLC
78 East Industry Court
Deer Park, NY 11729

ISBN 13: 978-1-60162-857-2
ISBN 10: 1-60162-857-9

First Printing June 2010
Printed in the United States of America

10 9 8 7 6 5 4 3 2 1

Distributed by Kensington Corp.
Submit Wholesale Orders to:
Kensington Publishing Corp.
C/O Penguin Group (USA) Inc.
Attention: Order Processing
405 Murray Hill Parkway
East Rutherford, NJ 07073-2316
Phone: 1-800-526-0275
Fax: 1-800-227-9604

I have to send a shout out to my girls in the Anointed Authors on Tour, I wish every one of you all the success in the world.

Also by Vanessa Miller

Former Rain
Abundant Rain
Latter Rain
Rain Storm
Through The Storm
Forsaken

Dedication

This book is dedicated to my sister, Debra Clark.
May you always trust God and never look back.

Prologue

Crouched down between a rusty old Lincoln with a playboy symbol on the driver's side door and a red Pontiac with a busted rearview window, while a maniac wielded a tire iron that had already clipped her in the leg once, Diane Benson decided it was time to call her husband and beg for his forgiveness.

She had left Cleveland, Ohio about eight months ago after leaving her three oldest children with her husband, Joe Benson. She then drove to Pastor JT Thomas's house and left her three-month-old daughter with him and his wife. The way Diane saw it, every child needed to be with his or her own daddy, and she didn't care how JT and Cassandra's life was disrupted. JT got what he deserved anyway. What kind of man pastors a church while sleeping with the deacon's wife? But JT hadn't only been sleeping with her. Diane could have understood if he had slipped into sin because he just couldn't resist her voluptuous curves and Angelina Jolie pouty lips. But that hadn't been the case.

JT would sleep with anything in a knee high skirt willing to kick off her pumps and get busy. Too bad she got pregnant before she figured that one out. She had been prepared to leave her husband for JT so they could start a new life with their baby. But JT suddenly developed a conscious and realized that a husband's place was at home with his wife. He expected her to just continue living a lie with Benson. JT never imagined that she would tell Benson the truth. But she had, and Benson beat the snot out of him.

Soon after JT got his beat down, Diane had become fed up with the whole matter. So after dropping Lily off with her daddy, she left town with Brian Johnson. Brian had been the mechanic at the auto dealership her husband owned. But Brian was fixing more than automobiles, and Joe hadn't had a clue about it. Brian had been her sidekick. When JT wasn't acting right, she spent her free time with Brian. She may have imagined herself as first lady of Faith Outreach while fooling around with JT, but Brian was the one who made her weak in the knees. She couldn't lie if she wanted to; that man held some type of demonic power over her, and she lived to do his bidding. Actually, Lily could have been Brian's baby just as well as JT's. But Brian said that since she had been sleeping with JT more than him around the time that she'd gotten pregnant, Lily more than likely belonged to JT. Funny thing was, when the DNA test came back and it proved that Brian had been right; JT was Lily's father, Brian got so mad that he up and left her in Jacksonville, Florida with only twenty dollars to her name.

That's when she met Darryl Mills. Darryl was a house flipper. Since the economy turned and not many people were buying homes, he'd given Diane the key to a fabulous four bedroom home in the suburbs. Diane loved the house and was trying to figure out how she could convince Darryl to give it to her instead of putting it back on the market. Diane almost had Darryl convinced, until his nosy wife figured out that she was living in the house rent free. That's why Diane was crouched between two cars right now. The maniac with the tire iron was Darryl's wife.

"You might as well come out from between these cars. 'Cause I really don't care if I bang these cars up, just as long as you get banged up in the process."

Crawling on the ground, trying to move farther into the jam packed parking lot and away from the tire iron, Diane said, "I don't even know you, lady. Why are you doing this?"

"You know me well enough to sleep with my husband," the woman said as she angled her obese body between the two closely parked cars and swung at Diane.

Thankful that the woman missed her that time, Diane stood up and ran as quickly as she could through the maze of cars.

Darryl's wife was simply too big to move any farther in between the Lincoln and the Pontiac, so she couldn't catch Diane, but she screamed as loud as she could, "I'm throwing all your stuff out of my house and onto the street. If you come back here to get any of it, I'm going to shoot you."

Once Diane was a safe distance away from certain death, she used the cell phone that Darryl bought her to call Benson. When he answered she said, "Hey, Joe, I was just calling to check on the kids. How are they doing?"

"They miss you, Diane, that's how they're doing," Joe told her.

"I know. I know," she said, like a woman who'd learned her lesson. "I should have never left them. I miss all my babies."

"You received court papers about a custody hearing for Lily last week."

"What?" she said as if she couldn't believe this was happening to her. "What am I supposed to do, Joe? I don't even have a way to get back to Cleveland right now."

"The hearing is next month. I'll get you an airline ticket. Just tell me where you are."

That's what she wanted to hear, but she tried to tamper down her excitement as she said, "I don't know, Benson. The only reason I didn't turn around and come right back home eight months ago was because I was scared about how you would treat me."

Benson was almost seven feet tall, bulky and strong, but with his wife, he might as well have been a midget. "Have I ever given you a reason to fear me? It's not just the kids missing you, Diane. I miss you. Just come home."

"What about Lily? I can't just forget that I have another child."

"I wasn't sure that you wanted Lily since you left her with JT."

"She's my child," Diane said angrily. JT wasn't just going to run over her with some custody hearing, telling some judge that his wife would be a better mother than she was.

Benson cleared his throat. "Just come home, Diane. We can work on getting Lily back from JT once we're back together."

"Okay, Benson. I'm in Jacksonville, Florida. Go online and order the ticket, and I'll pick it up at the airport." Diane smiled as she hung up the phone. Benson had always been at her beck and call. She would go home, but she would also make JT pay for the agony she felt had been inflicted on her because of his refusal to leave his wife and marry her. And she would start by taking Lily away from him.

One

"What are you doing?" Mattie Davis asked when she walked into her daughter's bedroom and saw her throwing her clothes into a suitcase.

Cassandra Thomas turned to face her mother. With a smile on her face she said, "I'm going home."

Looking heavenward, Mattie proclaimed, "Lord Jesus, my child has lost her mind again." Mattie sat down on the edge of Cassandra's bed. Her head was bowed low as she shook it from side to side. "Why do you want to ruin your life? I don't understand this at all."

"Stop being so dramatic, Mother. I've been away from JT for six months. It's time I went home."

JT Thomas had once been the pastor of Faith Outreach Church, but once his sins had been exposed, he'd been suspended, and then he resigned from his position. JT was now restored back to God and an upstanding citizen who went to work at a community center everyday and held a monthly Bible Study in his home for men struggling with infidelity, and he'd also just started his own church. And yes, Cassandra was willing to admit it; she had fallen in love with her husband all over again. So why shouldn't she and her two sons, Jerome and Aaron, go back home where they belonged?

"I suppose this means you're willing to be a mother to that child he had while still married to you," Mattie stated.

"Yes, Mother, I will be just as much Lily's mother as I am Jerome and Aaron's. I've thought long and hard about this, and the way I see it, if another woman was willing to be a mother to me after you and Bishop Turner fooled around and had me, then how can I deny a child my love, just because I didn't give birth her?"

Mattie's shoulders' slumped. "You enjoy throwing that in my face, don't you? Okay, I made a mistake. Your father was a married man. But does that mean you have to pay for my sins for the rest of your life?"

Cassandra sat down next to her mother and put her arm around her shoulder. Her mother was a petite woman of little more than five feet, but she had a loud, boisterous voice that made her seem seven feet tall at times. "I'm not trying to throw anything in your face, but I'm in a predicament, and I need your help to get out of it."

"What predicament? What are you talking about?"

"Well, it seems to me that you and Bishop Turner did to Susan what JT and Diane Benson did to me. Susan forgave you and Bishop and found a way to continue loving his wife. All I'm asking for is the chance to do the same thing with my husband."

"But how can you forgive what that man has done to you?" Mattie asked, refusing to see that she had done the same thing to another man's wife.

"The same way that I forgave you for all the years you lied to me about who my father was. The way I see it, Mother, forgiveness is a choice." Cassandra stood up, zipped her suitcase, and pulled it off the bed. "Thank you for putting up with me and the boys for all these months, but I'm going home, Mother."

***

Cassandra put her key in the lock and opened the door. She stood in the entryway and looked around the modest home. It was certainly not the five bedroom, seven thousand square foot home she shared with JT before moving in with her mother. JT had sold their home after she moved in with her mother. He moved back into the first home they purchased together. It was only thirteen hundred square feet with three bedrooms and a basement, but Cassandra had loved everything about this home. Jerome and Aaron ran into the house and started screaming for JT.

When JT walked from the kitchen into the living room, the boys ran to him. He bent down and Jerome and Aaron jumped on him. "Daddy, Daddy, guess what?" Jerome said.

Laughing, JT said, "I can't guess, so please hurry up and tell me."

"We're home for good!" Jerome shouted.

"You are?" JT asked playfully.

"Yes. Mom said so." Jerome turned to Cassandra and asked, "Isn't that right, Mom? No more sleeping at Granny's house during the week and here on the weekends. We get to be here with Daddy all the time now, don't we?"

The excitement in her son's voice brought tears to Cassandra's eyes. How she wished that she had never moved him away from his father, but at the time, she had no idea that she would ever come home again. So she and JT had agreed on shared custody. Just as Jerome had said, she had the boys during the week and JT had them on the weekends. "Yes, honey, we are home for good."

JT smiled as he stood and walked over to Cassandra. "I made dinner."

"You did not," Cassandra said as she put down her suitcase

and walked into the kitchen. Not once, in the nine years she and JT had been married, had he ever volunteered to fix dinner. He expected his meals to be on the table the minute he was ready to eat, but he didn't bother to help with anything remotely related to kitchen duties.

As Cassandra lifted the lid on the skillet, JT said, "It's just Hamburger Helper."

"No," Cassandra said as she grinned from ear to ear, "what we have here is a miracle."

"Do you think the boys are ready to eat?" JT asked Cassandra.

"They haven't had anything since lunch, so I'm sure they're ready. What about Lily; is she sleeping?"

"Yeah. I put her down for a nap awhile ago though, so I'd better go check on her."

Cassandra put her hand on JT's arm as she said, "No, let me go check on her."

"Okay, if you're going to get Lily, I'll help the boys wash their hands."

"Mr. Helpful, huh? Be careful, JT, I just might get used to this," Cassandra told him as she headed upstairs.

Lily was sitting up in her baby bed. Her big brown eyes were filling with tears as she opened her mouth to proclaim that she was awake and didn't appreciate being left alone. Cassandra took her out of the baby bed and held her close as she rocked the screaming child.

"There, there, Lily, it's not that bad." Cassandra sat down in the chair next to Lily's bed and continued to hold the child until her sobs subsided. She saw JT's features in Lily, just as she saw them in Jerome and Aaron. Funny thing was, looking at Lily and knowing that JT was her father didn't bother Cassandra anymore. Now she knew for sure that she was ready to be a mother to Lily. She began to sing to her, *"There's a Lily in the valley and you're bright as the morning star."*

JT hollered up the stairs, "The boys are starving, are you two coming down so we can eat?"

"Sounds like your daddy is starving and trying to blame it on the boys." Cassandra bounced Lily on her lap, and then said, "Come on, honey, let's go eat."

JT was standing at the bottom of the stairs waiting on them. "What were you two doing up there?"

Cassandra rubbed JT's stomach as she put her feet on the bottom step. "Sorry, I forgot how hungry you get."

"I'm a growing man. I need to eat on the regular."

The boys were seated at the octagon shaped table that was only big enough for four chairs. Cassandra placed Lily in her high chair, and then told JT, "We need to pick up Aaron's high chair from my mother's house in the morning. He really isn't big enough to sit at the table." Only six months had passed since she last lived with JT, so the children hadn't grown all that much. Jerome was now four years old, Aaron was eighteen months and Lily was ten months.

"Yeah, he does look a little awkward in that chair," JT said as he watched his son's legs dangle in the air. They were about two feet away from the ground, so there was no way that Aaron would be able to get out of that chair without help. JT put a plate of Hamburger Helper in front of each child.

"You help Aaron, and I'll feed Lily," Cassandra told JT.

Dinner was a big hit. The boys absolutely loved it. Lily's noodles and hamburger pieces had to be chopped up, but she loved the meal as well. After dinner, the family watched TV in the family room until bath time. Cassandra was bathing Aaron and Lily when JT walked into the bathroom with her suitcase.

"This was still by the front door. Does it have the boys' stuff in it or yours?"

Cassandra pulled Lily out of the tub and started drying her off. "Some of my clothes are in that suitcase. I knew the boys had clothes here, so I figured we could go pack up their stuff together."

"That's fine. I'll just put your suitcase in our bedroom."

Alarm registered on Cassandra's face. She lifted her hand to halt JT. "Let me finish up with the kids before we make any decisions."

With a raised eyebrow, JT said, "What decisions?"

She finished drying Lily, handed her to JT, and then took Aaron out of the tub and dried him off. "Let's put them to bed, and then we can talk."

They put on the kids' pajamas, and then laid them in their beds. Jerome had already bathed and was sound asleep. JT grabbed Cassandra's hand and pulled her out of Jerome and Aaron's room. "Let's talk."

They walked into their bedroom. Cassandra saw her suitcase in the corner and froze. JT gently pulled her the rest of the way into the room. "What's wrong?" JT asked.

"Nothing's wrong, I just thought that we might want to wait a little while before I moved back into our bedroom."

"Where are you going to sleep, Cassandra? We only have three bedrooms in this house, and they're all taken."

Wringing her hands and looking everywhere but at JT, Cassandra said, "I thought I would sleep in the room with Lily for a little while."

JT sighed as he let go of Cassandra's hand and sat down. He looked at his wife as he said, "That's not going to work for me, Sanni."

There had been a time when Cassandra had asked JT not

to refer to her as Sanni anymore. That nickname meant a lot to Cassandra. It made her feel special and like she really mattered to JT. When he had done all his dirt, she no longer felt special, but times were different now.

"I don't plan to sleep in Lily's room forever. I just want to make sure this is going to work between us," Cassandra reasoned.

JT shook his head as he stood up and walked toward Cassandra. He put her hand in his. "I want a real marriage, and that includes you sleeping in here with me."

"But... but what if something happens? What if we can't make a go of this?" Cassandra asked with fear in her eyes.

"I know I let you down before, Sanni, but I'm a different man now. I will never hurt you like I did before."

What had Cassandra said to her mother earlier? Something about forgiveness being a choice? Maybe trust was a choice also. Maybe she needed to throw caution to the wind and just lean in. She wanted to forget about the past and move forward with JT as if nothing had ever gone wrong in their relationship.

When she didn't answer, JT said, "Have a little faith, baby. We are going to make this work."

Mattie was screaming inside Cassandra's head, telling her to look before leaping. She tried to deny the voices in her head and go with the feeling in her heart. "Okay, JT," she said. "We will have a real marriage." Cassandra then closed her eyes and allowed herself to be swept into JT's arms. She loved this man and wanted to spend the rest of her life making love to him. Cassandra silently prayed, *Please, God, if this is a dream, don't let me wake up.*

Two

JT woke up frustrated, just as he had for the last month since Cassandra moved back in with him. He looked over at his wife and smiled as he noted that she was still in bed with him. But the smile quickly dissipated as he realized that his wife had now been back in his bed for twenty nine days and they still had not consummated their reunion.

He believed her when she said that she wanted to make love with him. But when they would get down to it, Cassandra would have a panic attack. And what man wanted to make love to his wife after she freaked out from his touch. So again this morning, JT was leaving his bed unfulfilled, but determined to hold on.

He couldn't blame Cassandra for the way things were between them now. Heck, if she had been the one sleeping around, and then one of her former lovers stabbed him, JT couldn't honestly say he would have forgiven Cassandra, let alone reconciled with her. Not that he was mentioning any of that to his wife. He was just grateful that he had been the one to receive forgiveness rather than the one who had to give it. He didn't know what he would have done, and he never wanted to find out.

JT jumped in the shower, and then went into his office to read his Word and commune with God before his family woke up. He had always been an early riser, but now he used his time to seek the Lord's guidance for his life rather than sneaking in an early morning booty call. "Thank you, Lord," JT said as he bowed his head. "You have blessed me with a wonderful family. I just wanted you to know that I appreciate them a lot more these days." JT continued praying and reading his Bible for almost an hour. He then went into the boys' room to wake them up.

Tuesday was Cassandra's day to herself, so JT dressed the children and took them over to Cassandra's mother's house. Actually, he only took Jerome and Aaron to Mattie, the wicked one, because Cassandra's mother absolutely refused to watch Lily. JT's heart still ached over the conversation he'd had with Mattie the first time he dropped the kids off at her house.

"Only legits can stay here," she had said.

"Excuse me?" A look of confusion crossed JT's face as he attempted to carry Lily inside Mattie's house.

Mattie pointed at his daughter and said, "I'm not watching her."

"But I thought you told Cassandra you would keep the children on Tuesdays so that she could have some time to herself?"

"I sure did say that I would watch Cassandra's children. She deserves a break after putting up with you all week long. But I did not, under any circumstances, say that I would do a favor for the likes of you."

"I don't want to take Lily back to Cassandra, Mattie. This is supposed to be her day of rest." JT tried to reason with Mattie one more time.

With scorn and contempt in her eyes, Mattie said, "Look here, playa-playa, I'm sure you have a chick on the side who can watch ol' illegit, so that my daughter can have a break from your nonsense."

JT was so tired of his mother-in-law. She had the audacity to stand there and preach about Lily not being legitimate when Cassandra's father was a married man also. She was a hypocrite, and JT would have loved nothing better than to enlighten her to that fact. But it wasn't worth the argument he and Cassandra would have later once Mattie, the wicked one, told Cassandra what he'd said to her. He turned away from Mattie and said, "Her name is Lily, not illegit."

"Whatever," Mattie yelled at JT as he walked to his car. "Don't bring her over here no more and you won't have to worry about me calling her nothing."

JT wanted to pull his boys out of Mattie's house. The venom escaping that woman's mouth was toxic, and he feared what Jerome and Aaron might be internalizing it. But Cassandra said that the boys loved their grandmother and would be devastated if they couldn't spend time with her. JT had his doubts, but he'd left with Lily that day and never brought her back.

An elderly woman at JT's new church agreed to watch Lily on Tuesdays for a hundred dollars a month. Ms. Shirley Miller had been struggling financially since her husband passed. She'd lost weight because the food stamps given to her by the government didn't allow for a full month's worth of food. The last couple of days of the month, Ms. Shirley had nothing but soup and crackers if she had that. Even though money was now scarce, JT didn't mind parting with a hundred dollars a month for Ms. Shirley. The woman had filled the roll of a grandmother for Lily, and for that he would forever be grateful.

JT got the children dressed, and then went back into his bedroom, kissed Cassandra on the forehead, and then left the house. When he got in the car, he realized that he didn't have his cell phone, so he rushed back into the house to get it. If Cassandra couldn't get in touch with him, she always left him messages that tore at his heart. It wasn't so much what she said on his voice mail, it was the fear he heard in her voice. As if she were picturing him someplace he didn't belong – like with another woman, while she was leaving the message.

He'd tried to reassure her. But no matter how she tried to hide it, JT saw the worry in her eyes. So he limited time away from home and answered the phone when she called no matter what he was doing. At times he felt like a prisoner, but he'd do whatever it took to win back Cassandra's trust.

He dropped Lily off to Ms. Shirley first. Even though Lily was still too young to understand grown up conversation, he never wanted Lily to hear the things Mattie, the wicked one, said about her ever again.

However, the boys were a different story. They got to watch their father get criticized on the regular. JT had had his fill of Mattie's antics. He'd already told Cassandra that if Mattie pulled another one of her stunts, he would not leave the boys with her. "Okay, boys, we're here," JT said with a fake smile on his face as he parked in front of his monster-in-law's house. He unbuckled Jerome and Aaron, and then walked them to the front door.

Mattie opened the door with a broom in her hands. She looked at Jerome and Aaron and said, "Hurry up, boys; run in the house so I can sweep this devil off my porch."

Fed-up, JT held onto his sons as he turned back around and started walking toward his car.

"Where are you going with my grandchildren?" Mattie demanded.

JT turned back around and told her, "I'm not going to allow you to fill my children with hate. I will find someone else to watch them."

"You can't take my grandchildren away from me. Not after I went through twelve hours of labor bringing their mother into this world."

JT put his sons in the car and buckled them back in. "This is it, Mattie. I've allowed this to go on for far too long as it is." He closed the passenger side door and walked around to the driver's door.

"So you're back to wearing the pants in the family, huh? You done spent a month kissing and making up to Cassandra, and now you think you got the power to take my grand kids away. Well, I got news for you... It will take a lifetime for you to make up for all the sleeping around you did on my daughter. Do you hear me, JT?" Mattie held the broom in the air as if it were a spear that she was aiming at JT's heart. "You got a lifetime of mess to make up for."

JT got in his car without saying another word to Mattie.

From the backseat, Jerome asked him, "Daddy, why do you act like the devil when we go to Grandma's house?"

JT shook his head, feeling powerless. "Son, I'm not sure why your grandmother said that. But I try real hard not to act like the devil."

"That's not what Grandma says. She told us that she treats you so mean because you always acting like the devil."

JT put the key into the ignition as he watched Mattie walk her hateful self back into her house. "I don't really think your grandmother means the things she says, Jerome."

"Maybe you're right," Jerome said as he leaned back in his car seat, and then continued. "Grandma says you're a cheat too, but I've never seen you cheat at anything."

Aaron picked that moment to laugh his head off. But JT didn't find anything funny. He wished that he could tell his sons that he had never cheated at anything in his life. But that wasn't true. He had cheated on his wife, time and time again. He broke Cassandra's heart and would probably never forgive himself for all the pain he inflicted on the one person he'd promised to love and cherish. But all that was in the past. As JT drove down the street, he declared that he was a new man now, and with the help of God, he would never be a cheat again.

Three

Stepping out of her bed, Cassandra stretched and yawned. Her body ached as if she had been lying on rocks all night long. The house was quiet as it normally was on Tuesdays. She wanted to climb back in bed, stretch out, and bask in the peace. But she had an appointment this morning that she couldn't reschedule.

She hurriedly showered and threw on a pair of no-name jeans, a purple and black striped turtle neck, and black pumps. Cassandra picked clothes that she liked and that looked good on her. She never concerned herself with labels. She was one of those women who looked like a million bucks in whatever she put on. Cassandra didn't need the help of designers to look model-fabulous.

The phone rang as she picked up her purse. Cassandra looked at the caller ID and almost didn't answer it. But then she reminded herself that she was trying to work this relationship out. "Hey," was all she said after lifting the receiver to her ear.

"Hey yourself," he said.

It was Bishop Turner, the man Cassandra had loved and adored because she thought he was her godfather. But last year she discovered that Bishop Turner was actually her father, and their relationship hadn't been the same since. "What's up?" Cassandra asked, trying to hurry the conversation along.

"Susan and I will be in town next month, and I was hoping that we could take you, JT, and the children out to dinner."

"I don't know," Cassandra said hesitantly as she tried to come up with an excuse. "JT's been working real hard trying to rebuild his ministry, so we might be busy when you come into town."

"He told me that you all had outgrown the basement and that the community center he works for was allowing him to use their gym for Sunday services."

Cassandra didn't respond.

"Well, I'll tell you what. I'll give JT a call and work out the details with him."

"Okay." Cassandra glanced at her watch, and then said, "Look, can I talk to you later? I'm running late for an appointment."

"All right, I'll talk to you later, baby girl."

She hung up the phone, gritting her teeth at the audacity of Bishop Turner. To refer to her as 'baby girl' was like slapping her. As a child she wanted nothing more than to be his little girl... used to pray about it every night. *Please, God, I wish Bishop was my daddy.* And all the time, he was, but nobody ever let her in on the secret. Now she understood why it had been so important to Bishop that he not only marry her and JT, but that he walked her down the aisle as well. Her wedding album was full with pictures of her and the bishop. How she wished that she had known he was her father on that day. It would have been so much more special to her.

Cassandra waved away those thoughts as she walked out of her house and got into her 2008 Mazda. She didn't miss the mansion size home she and JT owned less than a year ago, nor did she miss her Lexus or JT's Bentley that had been sold in order to pay off their debts. The way they used to live had never impressed her. She could take it or leave it; which ever way the wind decided to blow. Cassandra was content with what she had.

But content didn't mean happy. And lately, Cassandra wondered what happy looked like. She understood that she was living in a new reality. One in which her husband was no longer pastor of a prominent church in Cleveland, but was now rebuilding his church by using the gymnasium of the community center he worked at during the week as a Community Organizer and Youth Counselor. Her new reality also included a baby that JT had by another woman that she was now responsible for raising. But Lily wasn't the reason she was unhappy... right? The fact that she was now first lady to a twenty five member church, rather than the three thousand member one they were thrown out of, didn't really bother her... did it?

Cassandra couldn't pinpoint the reason she was having such a hard time adjusting to her new normal, and for that reason, she was now parking her car in front of Dr. Corey Clarkson's office. She turned off the ignition and found herself staring at the small unassuming yellow brick building. It was a one-story building that Dr. Clarkson shared with a dentist. There was only one door in the front of the building. Patients walked in and either went right to sit in the dentist chair, or left to lie on a couch and explain why life had stabbed them in the back. Cassandra opened the doors and went left.

Once a month, JT met with his boys, Pastor Max Moore and Pastor Samuel Unders. The three of them served as an accountability team for each other. Pastor Samuel Unders had been an Elder at Faith Outreach Church when JT was the pastor there. But after the scandal that his infidelity caused at the church, JT felt compelled to resign and Unders took his place. Pastor Max Moore was the founder of True Vine Church, a fellowship that strived to be in tune with the voice of God.

Mattie's house was right around the corner from the Marriott where he was supposed to meet Max and Sam. He wanted to take the boys back to Cassandra before going to the Marriott for breakfast, but he was already late. So he pulled up at the restaurant side of the hotel, took his sons out of the car and made his way into the restaurant. JT asked the waitress for a high chair and a booster seat, and then walked over to the table with his friends.

Max laughed as JT sat down. "Man, I knew this would happen. Cassandra's got you on such a short leash; you can't even have breakfast with your boys without bringing the kids."

"Shut-up, Max-a-million," JT said, using the name that he'd given Max a few months back when his congregation had grown to five thousand. Funny thing was, Max took the status of having a mega church in stride. He didn't puff up and start demanding stuff that even Jesus wouldn't ask for. Whether he had a million dollars or two dollars to his name, he was the same lovable guy as always, and JT admired him for that.

"Okay now, boys, don't start acting up before I can get a little coffee in me," Unders said.

At sixty-seven, Sam Unders was the oldest of the group. He provided the wisdom that JT and Max sometimes needed. While at forty-two, Max was closer to JT's age and served as JT's friend and confidant. "I'm sorry I'm late, Mattie couldn't keep the boys this morning," JT said.

Then Jerome added, "She thinks Daddy is the devil."

Max had been drinking some orange juice, but Jerome's comment made him spit it out. He looked at JT. "She really said that?"

JT playfully hit Jerome in the back of the head. "Thanks for spreading my business." He turned back to Max and said, "Every chance she gets, that woman is always downing me. I just couldn't take it no more. I told her that she wouldn't be watching our children anymore."

"Did you talk to Cassandra about this?" Unders asked.

"Man, the woman called him the devil... In front of his children. That's just something Cassandra's gon' have to understand," Max said.

"I'm with you, Max. I told y'all how she talked about Lily and refused to watch her," JT said.

"I would have gone off right then and there. You get extra points in heaven for not going to jail that day," Max said.

"I might have to agree with y'all on that one. I don't know what I'd do if someone attacked one of my children when they were helpless babies," Unders said.

They were saved and pastors of churches, but they still bleed if you cut them. And right now, JT was cut all up. He didn't know what to do anymore, didn't know how Cassandra was going to act—but he needed her to be on his side. Thinking out loud he said, "I'm taking the kids home after our breakfast, so we'll see what she says."

Max covered Jerome's ears, leaned over to JT and said, "Look, I know you're still trying to get some b-e-d-r-o-o-m," he spelled out bedroom just in case Jerome could still hear him and continued, "action going on, but there's only so much a man can take. You need to put your foot down on this one."

When Max let go of Jerome, he looked up at JT and said, "What did he spell, Dad?"

"He was talking to me, Jerome. Not to my nosey four-year-old son. Sit there and eat Mr. Max's toast until I order you something," JT said as he picked up the menu and found something he, Jerome, and Aaron could share. JT knew he wouldn't get full, but his funds stayed low these days, and he and Cassandra were getting used to being on a budget again.

The three men caught up on each other's lives and the things going on in their ministries as they ate breakfast together. JT couldn't talk about his personal issues because he had Jerome with him, and he knew that his son would repeat everything he said.

When they finished eating, JT gathered his sons, put them back in the car, and drove home to hand them over to Cassandra so he could go to work. He hated to bring the kids back to Cassandra on her free day, but he couldn't take the kids to Ms. Shirley right now—he just couldn't afford it this month. He took the boys out of the car, and they ran up to the front door. JT figured that Mattie had already called Cassandra, so she was probably in the living room waiting on him. He opened the door and hollered, "Honey, we're back."

When there was no response, JT ran up the stairs and went into their bedroom. But Cassandra wasn't there. He came back downstairs and looked on the refrigerator to see if she left him a message about an errand she had to run. No message.

"Can we go play in our room, Daddy?" Jerome asked for him and Aaron.

"Yeah, go ahead. I need to figure out where I'm going to take you guys for the day if Mom doesn't return soon," he said as he helped Aaron up the stairs.

As he was putting the child proof gate against the stairway his cell phone rang. He didn't recognize the number, so when he opened his flip phone and put it to his ear he said, "Cassandra, is that you?"

"One time when we were laying in bed together you called me Cassandra. I didn't like it then and I don't like it now," the caller told JT.

"Who is this?" JT demanded.

"You know, JT, I'm really offended that you don't know the voice of a woman you have shared so much with. I mean, after all, we do have a child together."

JT still didn't recognize the voice. So with an arched brow he said, "Diane?"

"Unless you've had more kids outside your marriage, I would say you can stop guessing?"

"Where have you been," JT wanted to know.

"Miss me?"

"Diane, you left Lily with us for eight months without calling or anything. What kind of mother does that?"

"Don't you start lecturing me, *Pastor*." She said the word pastor as if she were calling him a pimp or a drug dealer.

"What do you want, Diane?"

"Nothing much. I just called to tell you that I'm back in town and that Joe and I want you to bring Lily back home. We don't need you to babysit anymore."

"Over my dead body! You abandoned Lily, and I'm not about to give her back so you can leave her God knows where the next time you decide being a parent isn't a good fit for you."

"You listen to me, JT. You will give my daughter back to me. I won't have her living with you and your stupid wife. I want her back."

"Then you should have thought about that before you left her on our doorstep. I'll see you in court next month," JT said as he hit the END button to disconnect the call. JT shook his head at the audacity of Diane Benson. The woman was just as miserable as his monster-in-law. Neither of them wanted to see anyone else happy. How in the world had he allowed himself to get caught up with that woman?

Before he could ponder that question, his cell phone rang again. Looking at the caller ID, JT recognized the number. It was Lamont Stevens, his old friend, Jimmy Littleton's son. It had taken JT three months to locate Lamont, then another three months to even get the young man to talk to him. But a promise was a promise. JT owed Jimmy, and since Jimmy would be in prison for more than a decade, he'd promised to give Lamont what he owed Jimmy. JT flipped open his phone and said, "Hey, Lamont, what's going on?"

"Lamont's been in an accident, Mr. Thomas. He asked me to call. He wants to see you," the female voice on the other end of phone said.

This cannot be happening. JT raked his hand through his hair as he asked, "How is he doing?"

"Not good. I think you better get here tonight."

Four

As she sat on Dr. Clarkson's couch for the second Tuesday in a row, she wondered again how things had gotten this bad for her. She folded her hands in her lap and sat there waiting for Dr. Clarkson to say something that would give her reason to hope again.

"So how did things go for you and your husband this week, Cassandra?"

Cassandra didn't like the idea of having to see a psychologist, but she hated the thought of wasting money even more. So if she had to be in this office, she wasn't going to waste time playing games. She opened her mouth and told Dr. Clarkson, "Nothing has changed. JT has been loving and kind to me since I moved back home, but we still haven't been able to make love. I freeze up every time he touches me, and I don't understand it; I love my husband. I really want our marriage to work, so why am I pushing him away?"

"Have you had anymore panic attacks?" Dr. Clarkson asked her.

"Last night," Cassandra said in a timid, small voice.

"How did you feel when it happened?"

Wringing her hands together, Cassandra said, "Awful. JT thinks that I don't want to be with him in that way. And that's just not true, but I can't stop my body from freaking out when he touches me."

Dr. Clarkson wrote something on his notepad, he then looked over at Cassandra and asked, "Are you still angry with JT about the affair?"

"Which one?" Cassandra said, then lifted her hand. "I shouldn't have said that. It's just that JT has had multiple affairs, and even though I believe that he has finally changed, I still think about what he did. But if I were still angry with him, I wouldn't have moved back home."

"Then who are you angry with?"

Cassandra was sitting on the edge of Dr. Clarkson's couch, but she felt as if she should lie down and explore that question. Sometimes she was angry with her mom and Bishop Turner. They'd lied to her since the day she was born, and it wasn't until last year that she discovered the truth about a man she had adored as a godfather. But she knew they weren't the reason for her panic attacks.

She should be angry with Vivian Sampson, the woman who stabbed her after having an affair with JT. And she definitely should be angry with Diane Benson, the woman who left hers and JT's love child on her doorstep.

If the truth was told, Cassandra was still too numb to be angry with those two women. She looked at Dr. Clarkson with newfound knowledge in her eyes. "I told you about the ordeal I went through with not only my husband, but my mother and father several months back."

"Yes, you did."

"Anyone would be well within their rights to be angry at any of the people in my life. I thought I had forgiven all of them, but if I'm numb, how do I know if I've truly forgiven them?"

"That is what you need to figure out. It has been my experience that Christians feel that God is against anger. But sometimes you need to go through those emotions in order to not just play lip service with forgiveness."

"And that's what you think I'm doing? Just playing lip services with forgiveness?

"That's something you'll need to figure out. Look deep, Cassandra. There has to be a reason for your panic attacks."

All the way home, Cassandra kept trying to find her anger. She scrunched her eyebrows and concentrated on all the wrong that had been done to her over the years. She even went way back to old boyfriends and high school friends who had betrayed her trust. But still she couldn't muster any anger for any of it. Over the years she had perfected a dutiful silence that got her through the rough times with JT, but had she allowed her coping mechanism to turn her into a zombie?

As she pulled up to her house, she noticed JT's car in the driveway. She wondered why JT was at home. It wasn't even noon, so he couldn't be home for lunch. Cassandra parked next to JT's car, and then got out of her car.

JT opened the door, and as soon as she walked in, without saying hello, he demanded, "Where have you been?"

"Out," Cassandra said as she walked past him.

JT followed behind her. "Out where? Did you go to the grocery store or the mall?

Cassandra stopped walking and turned to face her husband. "What's the big deal, JT? I just went out for a while. Tuesday is my day, remember? So I can do what I want."

"I called your cell phone several times, but it keeps going straight to your voice mail."

Cassandra laughed. "Is that why you're acting like a murder has just been committed and I need to come up with an alibi? My phone died on me. I forgot to charge it this morning."

JT backed off and said, "Look, I didn't mean to jump at you. Something has happened, though."

Worry lines etched across Cassandra's forehead. "What happened? Is it one of the kids?" She ran to the phone and picked it up.

JT followed behind her. "The boys aren't at your mother's house. They're upstairs taking a nap."

She put the phone down and turned back to JT. "Nothing is wrong with Lily? Please, JT, don't tell me anything else has happened to that little girl." Cassandra had become very protective over Lily after she'd been kidnapped by JT's ex-lover, Vivian Sampson. But it was more than that. From the day Diane left Lily on their doorstep, Cassandra knew the little girl would have a special place in her heart.

JT gently grabbed Cassandra's hands and walked her over to the couch and sat down with her. "No, baby, nothing has happened to Lily. It's Lamont."

"Who?" Cassandra asked as if JT were speaking a foreign language.

"Lamont Stevens, Jimmy Littleton's son. You know, the one I've been ministering to for the last few months."

Recognition flashed in Cassandra's eyes. "The one you said seems to be following in his father's footsteps?"

"Yeah, well he's been in an accident. I don't know if it was a car or that motorcycle of his. The girl who called me said he's not doing too well. I need to get to New Orleans tonight."

"Oh, JT, I'm sorry. I know how much you wanted to help turn that kid around."

"God willing, I've still got time. But I need to leave you with the kids. Is that going to be a problem?"

"Go on to New Orleans, JT. I'll get my mother to help me with the kids."

JT lifted a hand as he shook his head. "That's another thing. I don't want your mother watching our children anymore."

Anger flashed in Cassandra's eyes as her hands went to her hips. "That's not right, JT. You already took Lily from her, now you want to take the boys away."

"Why do you choose to believe your mother over me? I didn't take Lily from Mattie, like she told you. She refused to keep Lily. As a matter of fact, she told me that no illegitimate children were allowed in her house."

Cassandra couldn't believe that her mother would say something like that. Not with the knowledge that she herself was illegitimate. "You misunderstood her, JT. There's no way she would say something like that."

"Did I misunderstand her this morning when she told my children that I was the devil?"

Cassandra's eyes bulged. "She said that?"

"And a whole lot more."

"Why didn't you tell me any of this was going on? She gave me her word that she would be nice to you."

JT lowered his head so that he wasn't making eye contact with Cassandra when he answered, "You haven't been acting yourself lately. I didn't want to add to whatever else has been stressing you."

Cassandra stood up and protested. "I'm fine. Just because I don't want to have sex doesn't mean I'm a mental case, and that I have to be treated gently so that I won't have a nervous breakdown."

JT stood. "I never said you were mental." He waved his hands in the air. "Look, I don't have time to have this discussion with you right now. I've already packed a bag, but I need you to pick Lily up from Ms. Shirley's. And please don't have your mother over here while I'm gone."

"Not a problem," Cassandra said while folding her arms across her chest. She had a couple things she wanted to say to him, but in traditional fashion, her mouth remained closed while the minion inside was balling its fist, aching for a fight. But what Cassandra didn't understand was why she'd chosen this moment to be upset with JT when he was only trying to go help someone.

JT picked his overnight bag up out of the hallway, walked back over to Cassandra, and tried to kiss her.

Cassandra turned her face away from his kiss and said, "I'll see you when you get back."

The look on his face questioned her, but he said, "I love you, Cassandra. I won't be gone long."

She walked him to the door without saying a word, but as she watched him pull out of the driveway, Cassandra picked up the phone and called her mother. She asked her to come hang out with her for a couple of days. JT wouldn't like it, but she didn't care. Cassandra hung up the phone thinking, *I really need to do something about my passive-aggressive behavior.*

Five

JT arrived in New Orleans a little before five o'clock that evening. He took a cab to Charity Hospital. When he was dropped off, he ran straight to the visitor's station and asked for Lamont's room.

"He's in ICU, sir. Only family can see him right now."

"I'm a clergy," JT told the woman. "His family called and asked me to come see him."

"Let me call the nurse's station on his floor." She picked up the phone, dialed, and then turned her back to him as she spoke on the phone. When she hung the phone up, she turned back to JT and gave him the room number.

"Thanks," JT said as he ran toward the elevators the woman directed him to. He didn't know how much time Lamont had left, but he knew for sure that the boy was still alive. The nurse on Lamont's floor wouldn't have okayed his visit if Lamont was dead.

As JT jumped off the elevator on Lamont's floor and looked for the direction he needed to go in order to find the room, he heard loud, painful sobs. He hated that anyone was in that much pain, but he prayed that those sobs were not for Lamont.

He'd promised Jimmy that he would look after his son, help him become a better man than either he or Jimmy turned out to be. Lamont was only nineteen years old. His entire life was in front of him. JT just couldn't accept that this might be the end.

As he turned the corner, he bowed his head respectfully to the men and women lining the walls of the corridor with tears streaming down their faces. One teenage girl, with fat cornrows in her head, slid down the wall as she screamed, "Why, God? Why her?"

JT wanted to go to her. He wanted to reach out to each and every one of them, but his place was two doors down the hallway. No one stood in front of Lamont's door. If the woman who called him could be believed, the boy was close to death. Where were his loved ones?

He opened the door to Lamont's room and found it to be just as empty inside as out. Only Lamont was in his room. He probably would have left himself, if he hadn't been tied to an IV and oxygen tank. As JT stood beside Lamont's bed, he realized that he could have just as easily been looking at Jimmy when the two of them were nineteen. He had those same bushy eyebrows and wavy hair that Jimmy used to say drove women wild.

The girl who'd called said that Lamont had asked for him just before going into surgery. JT looked at his watch. Lamont had probably been out of surgery for three or four hours now, but he was still knocked out. And if the monitor observing his heart rate was telling the truth, he wasn't doing too good. JT put his hand in Lamont's and gently squeezed it. "Hang in there, man. Don't give up."

JT's cell phone rang. He took it off the holder hooked to his jeans and looked at the caller ID. It was Lamont's number again. He pushed talk and said, "Hey, where are you?"

"I had to get out of there. Shameka's people showed up, and I didn't want to be on the same floor with them when they found out she was dead."

"Who is Shameka? What's going on?" JT asked. But before the girl could answer, Lamont's door swung open and banged against the wall. The sound was so loud that even in his coma-tose state, Lamont flinched.

This huge man, about six-nine, stood in the doorway with nostrils flaring. He was staring at JT the same way Deacon Benson had stared at JT when he attacked him for fooling around with his wife. But this giant's anger wasn't directed at JT.

"Move out of my way, I'm going to kill him," the man said as he stomped his way into the room.

Caught off guard, JT stumbled backward. His foot got tang-led in the cords. As he tried to extract his foot from the cords, he unplugged Lamont's heart monitor. The big man advanced on JT and tried to push him away from Lamont. Leaning against Lamont's bedrail with his hands outstretched, JT tried to keep the big guy from knocking him to the ground. "Hold up. Wait a minute!" JT yelled authoritatively.

The man stood in front of JT. All though he was no longer trying to push JT out of the way, he was clearly still as angry as sin. "He shouldn't have rode my sister on that motorcycle of his."

JT righted himself as he prepared to stand in the gap for Lamont's life. He waved his hand toward Lamont and told the man, "Can't you see that he's at death's door himself?"

At that moment, a nurse ran into the room. "What's going on in here?" she demanded.

JT didn't want to cause this man any trouble. He saw the pain in his eyes and knew from what he had said that his sister was dead. "You don't want to do this," he said to the big guy, and then turned to the nurse. "This man is upset. He just lost his sister. Can you please get some help so we can calm him down?"

"JT?" the nurse asked.

JT hadn't looked at the nurse when he spoke to her a moment ago. He was too busy trying to keep this big guy off of Lamont. This time when he turned toward the nurse he looked at her and recognition hit him in the gut. "Erica?"

"Yeah, it's me. I'm going to get security, and then I'll be back," she said as she backed away from the door.

JT looked at the man. He could barely concentrate on him. Images of his first love, Erica Swell, danced through his head and made him a little incoherent. He shook his head, trying to release the past so he could concentrate on the angry man standing in front of him. "You don't want to go to jail do you?" JT asked the guy.

The man pressed his palms against his head and let out a loud roar. "I want my sister back," he said as tears streamed down his face.

JT pulled the man into his arms and embraced him as if he were a two-year-old child in the middle of a tantrum. "It will be all right. You've just got to have faith and believe that God can see you through this."

The man pushed JT away from him. "Go 'head on somewhere with that religious stuff." He walked toward Lamont's door, and then turned back around. He pointed where Lamont lay still unconscious and said, "You better hope he dies, because if he doesn't, I'm going to kill him with my bare hands."

JT had no doubt that the big man could do exactly what he threatened. He bent down and plugged Lamont's heart monitor back in, then turned back to Lamont as the giant left the room and prayed, "Lord, help Lamont get out of this situation and to learn to live for you. I speak peace over this young man's life. In the name of Jesus, victory will be his."

After praying over Lamont, JT sat down in the chair next to his bed and took his Bible out of his duffle bag. Just as he was getting comfortable, the door burst open again, but this time it was Erica, backed up by two bodyguards. "He left, huh?" she said as she looked around the small room.

JT sat up and put his Bible in his lap. "Yeah, I don't think he wanted to go to jail."

Erica smiled as she said, "We're going to post a guard at his door for the night."

"Thank you," JT said as he stood up and walked over to her. JT hadn't seen Erica in twenty years, but she hadn't changed much at all. She was still as pretty as ever with long hair that flowed down her back. She had it in a ponytail now. "How have you been? I didn't know what became of you."

She posed in her Sponge Bob smock and said, "Now you know. What about you, JT? The head nurse approved a clergy to stay in the room with Lamont. That can't be you?"

"In the flesh," JT said with a smile.

"Well, I'll be. I've wondered what happened to you many times, but I never pictured you as a preacher. God is good."

"Yeah, I figured that out."

"Well, I've got to get back to my other patients, but it was nice seeing you," Erica said as she turned to walk out of the room.

"It was nice seeing you again, Erica. I've thought about you so much over the years," he said before she was out the door.

"I've wondered about you too, so I'm glad I got the chance to see you again. Since you know the Lord, may I suggest you pray hard for this boy? He's going to need Jesus to get through the night." She pointed a finger in the direction of the hall, and then said, "That girl who just died two doors down was riding on his motorcycle without a helmet, and her family is fighting mad."

"I know. I just met the brother of the dead girl," JT said.

Erica waved him off. "Just be glad the mother didn't come in here. She probably would have slit his throat before I got a chance to ring the guard station." She walked over to the white board that was on the wall, erased a name, and then wrote hers. She turned back to JT and said, "I'll be here the rest of the night with Lamont."

"Lamont doesn't appear to have any family with him. So do you mind if I spend the night here to make sure he doesn't receive anymore unwanted visitors?"

"We're posting a guard outside his door for a few hours, but I'm okay with you staying." She pointed to JT's Bible and said, "Why don't you read to him. That might help him to heal a bit better while he sleeps."

JT sat down and grabbed his Bible. But his mind was playing too many tricks on him to read a word from the Lord. Had he really just seen his first love after all these years?

Six

"Girl, why are you running around here like a Thanksgiving turkey being drug to the slaughter house?"

Cassandra had invited her mother to spend the night so that she would have help with the kids while JT was gone. Big mistake. "What are you talking about, Mother?"

They were in the kitchen. Cassandra was washing the dinner dishes while Mattie sat at the table drinking a cup of bitter black coffee. She put the cup down and told Cassandra, "Why don't you wake up and see what everyone else can see? You don't want to be here. And who would? That no count fornicator is God knows where, sleeping with God knows who, while you're left here to babysit his ill gotten seed."

Cassandra cringed at the way her mother spoke of her sweet baby girl. Because as far as Cassandra was concerned, Lily was just as much a part of her as Jerome and Aaron. There were days when she wondered if Lily had anything to do with the reason she was having panic attacks, but those questions quickly fell away when she held the little girl in her arms. Nothing that sweet could cause something so harmful.

"I need you to stop talking about Lily like that," Cassandra said as she put the last dish in the strainer, unplugged the sink, and then sat down at the table across from Mattie.

"Oh, so you don't allow no truth talking in your house, is that it, Cassandra Ann? Just act like everything is okay and then," she lifted her arms in the air and quickly flared her fisted hands and said, "poof, like magic everything will be as it should."

"You need to respect the fact that I love my husband and am—"

"I don't need to respect nothing," Mattie interrupted. "That fornicating husband of yours is the one who needs to respect your love."

Cassandra slammed her hand on the table and stood up. "He's not cheating on me. Stop saying things like that."

"Now look here, Cassandra Ann, I know you're not getting flip with me." Mattie stood up with her hands on her hips.

"When you say things like this, it really makes me wonder what Susan said about me when I was a child."

Mattie sat back down. "Susan has nothing to do with this."

"She has everything to do with it. I was the same child that Lily is . . . Born from an adulterous relationship. But Bishop and Susan took me in."

Mattie scoffed. "Those people never had to take you in. Not like you've done for Lily. They kept you on the weekends, big deal. Till this day, that man still hasn't admitted to anyone outside of his immediate family that you are his daughter."

One of the kids started crying. Grateful for the distraction, Cassandra went upstairs. She knew even before she reached the room that Aaron had awaken. His cries, which turned into screams, always alerted her that his nap was over. She didn't understand why some babies wake up peacefully while others always had to start a riot. But maybe Aaron was protesting the fact that he had to leave beautiful dreams to once again enter an unfair and cruel world. Cassandra wanted to scream herself awake sometimes too.

She opened the door to Jerome and Aaron's room, and

like she suspected, Aaron was sitting up in his Spiderman tod-dler bed screaming his head off. Jerome, thankfully, hadn't stirred at all. Cassandra put her finger to her lips as she tip-toed over to Aaron. She picked him up and rushed him out of the room. As they headed back downstairs, she rubbed his back and said, "Its okay, honey. Nothing to worry about, I've got you."

Aaron wiped his eyes, and then wrapped his arms around his mother's neck as if she alone could save him from the boogie man that chased him awake.

"Grandma Mattie is here. Do you want to see her?"

Aaron lifted his head off Cassandra's shoulder and smiled while vigorously nodding his head.

"Yeah, she wants to see you too."

Mattie met them in the hallway and took Aaron out of Cas-sandra's arms. "Hey my little man, I missed you all day today."

"I saw you," Aaron said, in that mumbled tone of a nine-teen month old.

"Yeah, but that mean old daddy took you away from me."

"Mother," Cassandra's tone was rebuking. "Don't talk about JT in front of my children."

"Whatever." Mattie waved her hand in the air and turned to walk into the family room with Aaron on her hip.

Cassandra shook her head, but followed behind them. The phone started ringing, so Cassandra picked up the receiver in the family room. "Hello." The line went dead so she hung it back up and turned on the television.

"Who was it?" Mattie asked.

"I don't know. They hung up." Cassandra picked up the remote and put the television on the developmental cartoon station for Aaron. Aaron jumped down from his grandmoth-er's lap and sat in front of the TV and watched the alphabet float across the screen.

"Why don't you and the boys pack your stuff and come back home with me?" Mattie asked.

Cassandra noted that her mother did not invite Lily as she sat down in the chair across from the couch Mattie was sitting on. "I can't just up and leave. I don't even know when JT is coming back home."

Mattie harrumphed. "You're back home less than a month, and that no-account is already out of town on a secret rendez-vous."

Cassandra rolled her eyes at that comment. "JT is at the Charity Hospital in New Orleans visiting the son of an old friend, Mother. Nothing more. I really need you to stop with all your accusations against JT. I'm having a hard enough time as it is adjusting to being back home."

"That's because you never should have come back here. You should have shook the dust of this bad marriage off your feet and kept on trucking 'til you found something better."

Mattie's words hit Cassandra right where she lived. She had wondered if she had come back too soon, or if she should have come back at all. Cassandra knew that she loved JT. But was he truly the best God had for her? At that moment, Cassandra was sure that if she listened to her mother long enough, she would go upstairs, pack their clothes and leave her husband. So she lifted her hand and said, "Mother, I need you to stop." She looked at Aaron as he sat glued to the television, and then added, "JT and I have asked you not to say these things in front of our children."

Mattie waved her hand, dismissing Cassandra's comment. "I've got another joke. Do you want to here it?"

Cassandra didn't know where her mother came up with so many jokes. But they were almost always offensive or something she didn't want to hear. "If it's anything like the jokes you normally tell, I don't want to hear it."

"You always say that, and then you listen to them anyway."

"That's because I'm in the room with you when you tell your offensive stories."

"Hush, girl, ain't nothing offensive about my jokes. Just listen," Mattie said as she looked over at Aaron to make sure he was still transfixed by the television. "Okay, it goes like this. The CIA is having this training for operatives. So they put this man in a room and the director hands him a gun and tells him, 'In order to be a CIA operative, you need to be committed and be willing to do anything we tell you to do.' The man had just been laid off his job, and he was a little crazy anyway, so he said, 'Sure, no problem.' The director then told him, 'I want you to kill the next person that walks into this room.'

"The director left, and when the door opened, the man's daughter walked in. The man put down the gun and left the room with his daughter. He told the director that he couldn't take the job. He would never shoot his own child.

"The next potential employee was a young woman. The director went over the same drill with her. He left her in the room with the gun, and then her mother walked into the room. The girl burst into tears, and like the man before her, she told the director that she could not do what they asked.

"The final woman to be tested that day stood in the room with the gun in her hand, when the door opened she saw that it was her husband. He closed the door, and then the director heard the gun go off three times. Then he heard another sound that he wasn't familiar with; clickety-clickety-clack, clickety-clickety-clack, clickety-clickety-clack. The woman opened the door and walked out. She handed the director the gun and asked, 'When do I start?'

"The director looked puzzled, then he said, 'Before I can process your papers I have to ask you something. When you were in that room I heard two different sounds. I'm familiar with the click sound of the gun, but what was that other noise?'

"The woman smiled and said, 'Well, when I shot him, I realized that you had put blanks in the gun. So I picked up a chair and beat him to death with that.'" Mattie held her stomach and began laughing so hard she rolled off the couch.

"See, I knew I didn't want to hear it," Cassandra said as the phone rang again. She got up to answer it while still shaking her head at her mother. "Hello." There was silence, and then Cassandra heard heavy breathing. "Hello, who is this?" she demanded.

The caller continued to take deep, seductive breaths, and then released them into Cassandra's ear.

"I'm hanging up if you don't say something." They kept breathing, so Cassandra hung up and returned to her seat.

"What was that about?" Mattie asked.

"It was stupid really. Whoever it was wouldn't say anything, just kept doing all this heavy breathing."

"Heavy breathing, huh?" Mattie said as she looked at her watch, then back at Cassandra. "It's six in the evening, do you know where your husband's at?" She was mimicking that popular commercial that used to come on years ago at eleven every night, asking parents if they knew where their children were.

Cassandra had been in high school when that commercial used to come on, and she and Mattie would laugh every night. The running joke between mother and daughter had been, *when your child has a strict 9:00 P.M. curfew, you always know where she's at.*

But Cassandra wasn't laughing now. Mattie jumped out of her seat as she watched her child sputter and gasp as she struggled to breathe. "What's wrong? Oh my God, Cassandra, please tell me what's going on."

"I . . . need . . . air," was all Cassandra could eek out as she held her throat and continued to gasp and struggle to breathe.

Aaron turned away from the TV and came over to his mother. "What wrong?" he asked, looking just as puzzled as his grandmother.

"Move, Aaron. Let me take your mother outside," Mattie said as she opened the sliding glass doors, ran back to Cassandra, stood her up and rushed her outside.

Cassandra breathed in the evening air and tried desperately to think soothing thoughts. JT had told her to quote the 23rd Psalm when a panic attack threatened. So that's what she did. She couldn't speak it, but her heart said, "*The Lord is my Shepard, I shall not want. He maketh me to lie down in green pastures . . . Yea though I walk through the valley of the shadow of death, I will fear no evil.*"

And that's when it hit her. Quoting the 23rd Psalm while her mother and son looked at her like she was a freak, she realized that Dr. Clarkson had been wrong. She wasn't angry. She was scared to death that her life was all a lie, that JT hadn't changed, and that she was going to wake from this dream and find the boogie man chasing her.

Seven

JT woke early the next morning. He hadn't had much sleep the night before due to the constant round of nurses that came in to check on Lamont. Every time that door opened he thought Erica would come into the room. But she never did. As he drifted off to sleep, he thought of the night he and Jimmy were held up in a hotel, hiding from Lester Grayson. JT had gotten shot that night as he and Jimmy ran from the dope house they'd attempted to rob. It was only by the grace of God that JT hadn't bleed to death that night, since he didn't get to the hospital until the next day. By the time JT was being admitted into the hospital, Jimmy was being booked for the robbery he'd attempted the next day without JT. That was where the two men parted company.

JT had been young and impetuous, but he'd never envisioned himself as a lifetime criminal. As a matter of fact, that wild night of thievery with Jimmy was the only time in his life that he had ever stolen from anyone. He had been angry about his mother's death and his first wife's betrayal, so he threw caution out the back door and went on a ride that would eventually cost him more than he wanted to pay.

But that was the reason he was standing at Lamont's bedside now. He still owed a debt to Jimmy. He promised him that he would look after his only son, and by God, that's what JT was determined to do. He bowed his head and prayed out loud. "Lord, thank you for allowing Lamont to make it through the night. Thank you for health and strength in his body. But most of all, Lord, I pray that you open Lamont's eyes. Help him to understand that to truly live, his life must be in your hands."

The door opened, and Lamont's nurse walked in. "I need to take his vitals," she told him.

JT stepped away from the bed so the nurse could handle her business. Looking at the white board, he asked, "Is Erica off duty?"

"Yeah, but don't worry. She told me that our patient had no family here, but that you were clergy." She took Lamont's blood pressure, and then turned back to JT. "His vitals are looking good. Once he wakes up we should be able to move him out of ICU and into a regular room."

"Thanks," JT said as he sat back down and prayed that Lamont would wake soon and be ready to listen to reason.

JT got the answer to part of his prayer an hour later. Lamont groaned, and then lifted his right hand and touched his hip bone. Lamont had scraped himself up pretty good, but he didn't have any broken bones. The surgeon had put a patch over the wound and Lamont was trying to rip it off.

JT jumped up and grabbed Lamont's hand. "Don't do that. You'll start bleeding if you rip your stitches out."

Lamont turned groggy eyes toward JT. Recognition flickered in his eyes as he said, "You...came?"

"What else was I supposed to do? Some woman calls to tell me that you were in a bad accident; did you think I would just sit at home and wait on someone to call back and tell me whether you made it or not?"

"You meant it, huh?" Lamont said, and then fell back to sleep before getting his answer.

But JT knew exactly what Lamont was talking about. It had taken JT three months after Jimmy had given him Lamont's name to track Lamont down. He'd flown to New Orleans immediately and met with Lamont's mother, Peaches. She reminded JT of his own drug addicted mother. One look at Peaches, and JT knew how Lamont had grown up. He could imagine how many times the boy went to bed hungry because his cracked out mother sold the food stamps to buy more drugs. He knew that the boy had lit candles on the numerous occasions the power company had turned the lights out for non payment, just so he could see clear enough to get to the bathroom.

He was there to deliver money to Lamont. The money he owed Jimmy was now supposed to go to his son since Jimmy would be doing at least ten-to-twenty more years behind bars. But JT couldn't give Lamont the money without educating him. Not with the current condition the boy was living in. The money would be gone within six months, and Lamont would have nothing to show for it. So he took the boy to lunch and told him about his past friendship with Jimmy.

Lamont had been uninterested, until JT told him that Jimmy asked that he give one hundred twenty-five thousand dollars to his son. "What? You're kidding, right?"

"Jimmy and I want to help you succeed in life."

Lamont opened his hands. "Well then show me the money." He threw his head back and laughed. "I can't believe that my old man actually came through on something for me."

"Jimmy is very serious about doing this for you. He thinks that you could even become President of the United States one day."

"Go 'head on somewhere with all that. Just give me the money, and I'll decide what I'm going to do with it."

JT shook his head. "That's not the way it's going down, Lamont. What you need to know is that I have a hundred and twenty-five thousand dollars with your name on it. But to get the money you'll have to come to Cleveland with me. Work with me for a year, and then I'm hoping that you'll use the money for college and to buy a home."

Lamont laughed in JT's face. "Look here, Mister, whoever you are. I ain't no college boy. And what do I need to own a home for? So some fat-cat banker can come and take it from me? I may only have an eleventh grade education, but I do watch the news."

"You didn't finish high school?" JT asked, and then rebuked himself. Hadn't he just met Peaches? Of course the boy dropped out of high school. He's probably been involved in every penny anti hustle New Orleans had to offer just to survive. Can't be a high school student and survive on the streets too. JT had almost dropped out of high school when he was a kid himself. But Eloise put down her heroine needle long enough to find an after school program for youth at risk. JT went to the program. The first week he met several guys that had dropped out of school and were just hanging around doing nothing but smoking dope. That wasn't what he wanted out of life, so he decided to finish school.

"What I learn on the streets is way more educating than anything them school books was teaching me."

"All right then. I've just added a third thing you need to do in order to get the money."

Lamont had this smirk on his face that said *there's always a catch* when he asked, "What's that?"

"You'll need to get your GED."

"What? Man, are you crazy, what do I need a GED for?"

JT had simply smiled and said, "You can't get into college without your GED."

Lamont got up and walked out of the restaurant without looking back. JT paid the bill, and then ran after him. "Wait up, Lamont. I drove you here, remember? Are you going to walk home?"

Lamont turned angry, accusing eyes on JT. "You got my hopes up for nothing, man. Where I come from people get shot for less than what you did to me today."

"I come from the same place you come from, Lamont. And I'm not selling you empty promises. Jimmy and I want you to have a future. Now are you coming back to Cleveland with me or not?"

"What business do you own in Cleveland?"

"I'm a preacher. I'm building God's church, and I could use your help."

Lamont looked heavenward and then turned back to JT with his arms crossed around his chest. "Now I know you're crazy. You tell my dad that I said, thanks for nothing as usual." Lamont turned to walk away from JT.

JT put his hand on Lamont's shoulder. "Wait a minute, son."

Brushing JT's hand off him, Lamont said, "Don't touch me. I'm not your son, and I'm certainly not the son of your jailbird friend."

JT pulled his wallet out of his back pocket, took out his business card, and handed it to Lamont. "If you change your mind, give me a call. I believe that God has something special for you. You just have to give Him a chance."

Lamont put the business card in his pocket and said, "If I'm in need of a Bible or a sermon, I'll give you a call."

"Whatever you need, Lamont, I promise I'll be here for you."

"Yeah, okay. Well, thanks for lunch," Lamont said as he turned and walked away.

JT had gotten Lamont's cell number from his mother, so even though Lamont never called him, JT checked on Lamont from time to time after that day. Their conversations were always quick, because Lamont, the high school dropout, always had some important business he needed to take care of. Each time JT would call, Lamont would say, "Is my check in the mail yet?"

JT would respond, "Are you ready for that plane ticket to Cleveland?" JT felt in his gut he was doing the right thing. Money in Lamont's hand at that time was like water going down the drain. So JT continued to hold out. Now he wondered if he had done the right thing. Maybe if he'd given Lamont the money three months ago, he wouldn't be standing next to his hospital bed now.

Lamont stirred. He turned on his side and faced JT. He watched JT for a second without saying anything. Clearing his throat, he asked, "You still need help in Cleveland, Mr. Preacher?"

"I sure do. I've been waiting on you to wake up so I could try to talk you into coming back with me again."

"All I want to do is check on Sonya, and then I'm out of here as soon as they release me."

Since Lamont's mother's name was Peaches, he had a feeling that the woman he wanted to check on was the very same one who'd died yesterday. He hated breaking this kind of bad news, especially while Lamont was trying to heal. But he didn't think he should let Lamont reach out to the girl's family, since they wanted to kill him. So he asked, "Is Sonya the person who rode on the motorcycle with you?"

"Yeah. Have you seen her? Is she all right? Has she been in here?"

JT chewed on his bottom lip for a moment. Jimmy should

be here. Why hadn't he thought enough of his kid to put down his gun and get a real job? If he had, another man wouldn't have to see his son through this difficult time. Jimmy would be here delivering the bad news. With the most companionate tone JT could muster, he said, "Lamont, I'm sorry to be the one to tell you this, but . . . Sonya died yesterday."

Lamont closed his eyes as a single tear rolled down his face. "Sonya's dead?"

"Yes, son, I'm afraid she is."

He shook his head. The pain in his eyes was unavoidable as he rubbed his temples as if he were suffering from a massive migraine. "She wanted to ride, but I didn't have an extra helmet, so I told her she couldn't. She jumped on my bike anyway, and I took off." "Sonya is . . . was my ex-girlfriend. But we've always been cool, more like sister and brother than anything else. I should have made her get off my motorcycle."

JT patted Lamont's shoulder, trying to bring him a semblance of comfort. "That's tough, Lamont. But it was an accident."

With sorrow, Lamont said, "I shouldn't have let her ride." They sat in silence for a while, and then Lamont asked, "How did you find out about the accident?"

"A woman called me. She was using your cell phone."

"That's right," Lamont said as if the light had just come on inside his brain. "My girl, Shameka, was out there with us. She got mad when Sonya jumped on my bike, so I thought she had left. But when I wrecked, she was right there. I must have asked her to call you or something."

"God didn't save your life for nothing, Lamont. It's time for you to figure out what you need to be doing in life and get on with it."

Lamont yawned as sleep tried to overtake him again. "You don't have to convince me, JT. Just before I woke up, I had a dream about second chances. I'm not sure why Sonya isn't alive, because I should be the one who died. She had goals and dreams. All I do is waste time with my other unemployed friends."

JT wanted to smile, but Lamont's change of heart came at the cost of a young girl's life. Nothing to smile about there. He sat with Lamont until he fell back to sleep, and then he went into the hallway to call Cassandra. He needed somebody else to be excited about the fact that Lamont had finally agreed to come back with him.

He dialed the house phone and Mattie answered. After taking a deep breath and exhaling he asked, "Can I speak to Cassandra, please."

"She ain't here," Mattie said, and then hung up the phone.

Why would Cassandra have that woman at their house? She didn't mean them any good whatsoever. Shaking his head, he dialed Cassandra's cell phone. It went straight to voice mail. JT hung up wondering why her phone was forever going to voice mail lately.

Eight

Thanks for meeting me, Dr. Clarkson. I really appreciate you spending your lunch hour with me," Cassandra said.

"It's no problem at all. It's not often that my patients offer to treat me to lunch."

Cassandra laughed. "I don't know if you can call this a treat. You made me meet you at Subway, and then you wouldn't let me pay."

"Yeah, but you offered, and like my mama always said; it's the thought that counts."

"You're too good to me, Dr. Clarkson."

"What's with this Dr. Clarkson stuff? We're not in my office. We're just two people having lunch. My first name is Michael. "

Cassandra giggled. "We might be two people having lunch, but I've still got problems. I had another panic attack last night, Dr.—"

He held up a hand.

"I mean, Michael."

"I thought you told me your husband was out of town last night?" Michael asked.

"He was. That's the reason I figured out what my panic attacks are all about. I'm not angry like you suggested. I'm scared."

"What did you have to be scared about last night?"

"Someone kept calling the house holding the phone. That used to happen a lot when JT was cheating on me. Thanks to my mother suggesting that JT was up to his old tricks again, I flashed back and that's when the panic attack started."

Michael took a bite of his turkey sandwich and leaned back in his seat. He chewed, wiped his mouth, and then asked. "This flashback . . . What did you see?"

Cassandra didn't seem to have much of an appetite. The whole while they'd been sitting there, she'd only taken one bite of her BLT. As she looked at it, she wondered why she'd even ordered anything. She hadn't felt like eating anything since last night, after the breather phone call. "I kept getting pictures of the women JT fooled around with. Each one of them just kept flashing in my head until I couldn't breathe."

"And you're not angry with your husband about those past affairs?"

"I had been angry with him. But I can see that he's changed. I really think I forgave him for all the things that happened in our past. It's just that fear keeps gripping me, and I don't know what to do about it." She picked up her sandwich, thought about taking a bite, but then put it back down. "Is it possible to forgive someone, but still not be able to live with them?"

Michael took Cassandra's hand in his as he answered, "Sometimes letting go is the best thing for everybody."

Cassandra squirmed in her seat. She was becoming increasingly uncomfortable as Dr. Clarkson, or Michael, as he'd asked to be called, held onto her hand and intently gazed at her. She removed her hand, stood up, and said, "I think I need to get back home. But thank you for seeing me."

Michael stood up with her and stammered as he said, "I-I hope I didn't make you uncomfortable just now. I just hope you'll think long and hard about whether you should have gone back to your husband."

"I will," Cassandra said as she and Dr. Clarkson began walking out of the eatery. That's when she saw Diane Benson standing in the checkout line, taking pictures of her and Dr. Clarkson with her cell phone. Dr. Clarkson opened the door for Cassandra to walk out, but she told him, "I'll call to make an appointment. I just saw someone I know."

Cassandra walked over to Diane and said, "What do you think you're doing?"

"Don't you worry about what I'm doing, Ms. Thang. You need to be worried about yourself."

"You don't have a clue what you're talking about."

"I know what I saw. And I captured it all on my picture phone."

Shaking her head, Cassandra turned and walked away. Diane jumped out of the line and followed her out the door.

"Well, well, I guess JT isn't the only cheater in the family, huh?"

"Get away from me, Diane," Cassandra said as calmly as she could.

"Oh, I'm going to do more than get away from you." She lifted her cell phone in the air. "With these here pictures, I'm going to get my daughter away from you."

"What are you talking about? You haven't even called us to check on Lily in eight months."

"I've called."

"When?" Cassandra demanded to know, and then realization struck her and she added, "Heavy breathing on the telephone doesn't equate to calling to check on your child."

"Check JT's cell phone records if you want to know how many times I've called. He and I talk *frequently*. But he didn't tell you that, did he?"

"You're lying."

"Why don't you check his phone records and find out. I just talked to him yesterday."

"Why are you so evil? I've never done anything to you."

Diane put one hand on her hip and used the other hand to point a finger in Cassandra's face. "You can be as weak minded as you want to be over that sorry man of yours, but I'm telling you right now that your days of playing mommy dearest to my child are numbered."

Cassandra wanted to break the finger Diane was pointing in her face, but with this woman threatening to take her baby away, she was becoming weak and afraid again. "Lily doesn't even know who you are."

"And whose fault is that? I bet you didn't even tell her you're not her mother. But that's all going to change once the judge sees these pictures of you out fooling around when you're supposed to be home with my child."

"Get away from me," Cassandra screamed as she bolted away from Diane. She felt another panic attack coming on and didn't want to look like a freak in front of Lily's mother. So she ran to her car and quickly unlocked the door. As she sat down behind the driver's seat she rolled her window down and began to chant, "The Lord is my Shepard . . ."

After about five minutes, Cassandra's breathing became normal again, and she was able to think on something other than the 23rd Psalm. These attacks were getting worse. Up until last night when her mother witnessed her having a panic attack, JT had been the only one to see her lose control like that. And now, she almost let Diane Benson put so much fear in her that she had another episode. Thank God she was able to get to her car before anyone saw her. She put her hand over her face and prayed, "Lord, please help me."

Cassandra wanted to make sure her nerves were calm before she went home to three screaming, hollering, and crying kids, so she decided to drive over to the mall and look around for a little bit. She reached into her purse to get her cell phone and discovered that it was dead again. She smacked her forehead with the palm of her hand, "Why do I keep forgetting to charge this thing?"

She put her cell back in her purse and drove toward the mall anyway. Cassandra was sure that her mother wouldn't mind hanging out with her grandchildren for an extra hour. She just hoped her mother was treating Lily right. Cassandra practically had to beg Mattie to watch her so she could go see Dr. Clarkson.

Diane was giddy with excitement. She had gold in her hand, and she planned to use it. She flipped through the pictures she had taken of Cassandra and her new man. The one she liked best was of the two of them holding hands. They looked so sweet. Diane quickly uploaded that photo, and then e-mailed it to JT's cell phone.

She laughed as the picture mail went through. She then turned on her car and drove straight home. She was delighted when she saw that Benson's car was still in the driveway. She just had to show him this. He always talked about how nice and sweet Cassandra was. Well now he would know that she wasn't the only one who had succumbed to temptation. Maybe now he would take that hurt puppy dog look out of his eyes that always appeared when he thought she wasn't looking. As far as Diane was concerned, Benson was wrong for that. If someone says they forgive you, they should just go on and do it. Stop holding grudges.

She gripped her cell phone in her hand. *This will shut him up*, she thought as she opened the front door. "Hey, Benson, where are you?" she yelled from the entryway.

Benson came out of the kitchen, drying his hands with the dish towel. "Hey sweetie, I was just finishing up those dishes for you."

There he goes again, always letting her know when she didn't do something she was supposed to do. Maybe this was his way of getting back at her for cheating on him. He was going to knit pick her to death. Diane smiled and said, "Thank you, baby. You're my hero."

A big grin crossed Benson's face as he kissed his wife on the cheek. "You know me, baby. I do what I can."

She grabbed his arm and pulled him toward the living room. "Come sit on the sofa with me. I've got something to show you."

"This must be good. You seem so excited."

"Benson, you don't even know the half of it." She waited until they were seated together on the sofa. She then pushed buttons on her cell phone until she was viewing her pictures. She handed the phone to Benson and said, "Look at this."

Benson took her phone and scrolled down until he had seen all ten of the pictures Diane had taken of Cassandra with some man that he didn't recognize. He handed the phone back to his wife and stood up. "Are you fixing dinner tonight or do you want me to do it," was all he said.

Diane's eyes bugged out. "Benson, did you see the pictures I showed you?"

"I saw them. I'm not sure why you took them, but I'm sure you have your reasons."

"You're darn right I have my reasons. When I show these photos to the family court judge, we'll be able to get Lily back."

His eyebrows crinkled in confusion. "How could Cassandra having lunch with some guy help us get Lily?"

Did she have to spell everything out for this man? "Don't you get it, Benson? Cassandra's having an affair."

"I think you'll need much more than those pictures to prove an affair," Benson said while walking back into the kitchen.

Diane got up and followed him. "Didn't you see that man holding Cassandra's hand?"

"I saw it, but there has to be some other explanation. Cassandra is not that kind of woman."

If he would have slapped her it would've hurt less. "What are you trying to say, Benson? What kind of woman cheats?"

Benson turned to face his wife. He walked over to her and put his arm on her shoulder as he said, "I didn't mean anything by that, Diane. I just don't think Cassandra is cheating on JT, that's all."

"Why do you think so much of her? Cassandra is human just like the rest of us. She has faults and flaws maybe you just can't see them."

He rubbed Diane's back as he said, "Maybe I'm not looking because it's none of my business."

Diane shoved Benson away from her. "Oh, it's our business all right. But if you can't be bothered to get your hands dirty, then I guess I'll have to do it myself." She stomped out of the kitchen and plopped back down on the sofa in the living room. She picked up the telephone and dialed. When it was answered she said, "What's up, Margie?"

"Nothing much. I just got back in from filling out some job applications. You know how it is in this economy. I just got laid off again."

Diane couldn't help the smile that crept onto her face. It

wasn't that she was wishing bad fortune on Margie, but if she was hard up for money, she might be more agreeable to the plan Diane tried to talk her into last week. "Yeah, it's hard times all over. Benson's worried that he might have to lay some people off."

"Well, I hope I find something soon," Margie said with a hint of sadness in her voice.

That's when Diane decided to go in for the kill. "You know, Margie, Faith Outreach Church has deep pockets, and they owe us."

"I don't know about all this, Diane. I've worked so hard to forget about all the sin I committed with JT Thomas. I don't know if I can drudge it back up again."

"That man wronged you. He wronged us. And I don't know how you can let him get away with what he did without making him pay. I sure can't. JT is going to get what's coming to him; mark my words."

"Even if you're right, and JT needs to get what's coming to him, I don't see how we'll end up with a penny. JT doesn't have any money left. They moved out of that big house, he sold his Bentley. The man is broke."

"I know he's broke, Margie." Geesh, she was so tired of having to explain everything to every dumb body. "But Faith Outreach is not broke."

"He doesn't work there anymore. JT has a little over twenty members in his church and has to rent space from the community center he works at for Sunday services," Margie said.

"I see you're still keeping tabs on the man," Diane said with a smirk on her face.

"I can't help but hear things, Diane. I do know a lot of the same people he knows."

"And how is that?"

"Because I went to Faith Outreach all the years, and he was the pastor there, of course."

"Exactly," Diane said triumphantly. "He began molesting you while he was pastor of Faith Outreach. And all the leadership there did nothing but turn the other cheek while JT was doing his dirt."

"I wouldn't exactly say he molested me. I'm trying to tell the truth to myself these days. And I have to admit that I did go willfully."

"Call it whatever you want. Molested gets you more money in court than to just admit you were sleeping around with the pastor. Think about it, Margie. This was a man of authority, and he made you believe that there was some divine privilege attached to sleeping with him."

"True," Margie agreed.

"That's a molestation of the mind. I had to leave my husband and be apart from my precious children because of what that man did to me. So I guarantee you, Margie, he's going to pay," Diane said as her front door opened and her seven-year-old daughter, Brittany, and nine-year-old son, Joseph Jr. walked in.

The kids put their book bags down in the entryway, and then Joseph turned to his mother and said, "I'm hungry. Can I have a snack before dinner?"

Diane waved him off and said, "Go in the kitchen and ask your father." She then turned her back on her precious children and continued her conversation. "So what do you say, Margie. Are you with me on this or not?"

"I guess you're right. The fact that JT was our pastor is probably the reason I fell so hard for him. Since he's supposed to be a man of God, he should have left us alone."

"Amen, sister! So are you with me?"

"Yeah," Margie said. "Let's do this."

Nine

Lamont had been moved to a regular room by early afternoon. He was in and out of consciousness because the pain medication they had him on kept him groggy. When he was awake, JT listened as Lamont talked about plans for his future and how he was now determined to be a better man than his father had been.

For some people, near death experiences don't faze them. But others wake up with a new outlook on life. The same thing happened to JT when he woke up in the hospital after Jimmy ran him down with a stolen car. JT made up his mind to change his life as he recuperated from his accident. The change didn't occur all at once, but JT had been determined. And now he listened as Lamont did the same.

About an hour later as JT sat in the chair next to Lamont's bed reading Bible versus out loud, the door opened and in walked a young lady with bright red highlights in her hair. She wore skin tight shorts with stilettos. JT hadn't figured out yet, how these young girls walked in shoes so high.

She stood bedside Lamont's bed, and with tears in her eyes, she told him, "I'm so glad you're awake, Lamont. I was worried that you weren't going to make it."

Although it was evident that Lamont had a long recovery ahead, he smiled as he told his friend, "I got nine lives, baby."

"Okay, Mr. Big Talk. You just better hope Sonya's people don't get to you," the girl told him.

"Yeah, I guess you're right about that," Lamont said humbly.

JT stood up. "I'll give you two some privacy."

The young lady turned to face JT. "I'm so sorry. Where are my manners?" She held out her hand. "I was so glad to see that Lamont was still breathing that I forgot to speak to you, sir. I'm Shameka Owens, the person who called you about Lamont."

JT shook her hand and said, "I figured as much."

"Thank you for coming to see about him. I was scared to death that one of Sonya's people was going to kill him before he got a chance to heal from his own wounds. But I figured with you being a man a God, and in here praying and all, that Lamont would be just fine."

"Well, we can definitely thank God that he made it." JT looked to Lamont and said, "Don't over do it. If you need to rest, just close your eyes and drift off. I'll be back up in a little while."

JT took the elevator to the first floor so he could get some lunch. After ordering a ham sandwich, he sat down at the table and opened his cell phone again. His intent was to call Cassandra, but then he noticed that someone had sent him a message.

"Hey you," Erica said as she stood next to his table with a tray of food in her hand.

"Hey yourself. I thought you had fallen off the face of the earth," JT told her.

"Is this seat taken?" Erica asked as she looked at the empty chair across from JT's.

"Nope, sit down."

"My little boy got sick last night, and my husband was frantic with worry, so I had to get someone to take over my shift."

"That's good to know . . . Not that your little boy got sick. I just thought you were trying to avoid me or something. Anyway, how is your son doing?"

Erica smiled. "Much better. My husband knows everything about history, but very little about a boy with the flu."

"Your husband is a teacher?" JT asked. Funny thing was he didn't feel the least bit jealous about the man that had obviously claimed Erica's heart. All a person had to do was look into her eyes when she spoke of her husband to know that she was in love. JT used to see that look in Cassandra's eyes. But he'd stolen that happiness from his wife with his infidelity.

"Professor of History," she answered, and then asked as she pointed to the wedding ring on his finger, "You and Mona still together?"

JT shook his head as he touched his ring finger. "That ended a long time ago." He then had the decency to show a glimmer of embarrassment as he said, "Look, I never got a chance to apologize to you for how bad I treated you."

Erica raised her hand to stop JT. "We were in high school . . . Too young to be in love in the first place. And anyway, Charles is the man I was supposed to marry. We've been together for ten years now, and I love him more each day."

"That's good to know. But just so you know, I *was* supposed to be in your life back then. You were the first person to ever tell me anything about God. And I want to thank you for that. About a year after you and I parted ways, I got into so much trouble that I had nowhere to turn. Then I remembered the things you told me about God, and I started praying."

Tears bubbled in Erica's eyes as JT related his news. She covered her face with her hands for a moment, and then looked at him with renewed joy. "You don't know how happy

I am to hear that. I prayed for you so much the first couple of years after we broke up. But I never knew what happened to you. I will admit, through the years, I envisioned that something awful had happened to you. I couldn't put my finger on it, but every now and then the Lord would remind me to pray for you."

"Well, let me be the first to tell you that your prayers worked. God saved me, but more importantly, He delivered me. These last five years have been rough for me and my wife."

"What's her name?"

Now it was JT's turn to smile when talking about a spouse. "Cassandra," he answered.

"I can tell by that big grin on your face that you love her quite a bit."

"I do. She's the woman God had for me," JT said with a smile that quickly evaporated as he finished. "I'm just not sure if she still thinks I'm the one for her."

Erica gently put her hand over JT's, gave it an encouraging squeeze, and then released it. "I'm sorry to hear that. Is there any certain thing you want me to pray about?"

Just a year earlier, JT would have taken offense at someone offering to pray for him in the manner Erica was doing now. He would have told them that he knew the Lord, and was well able to pray for himself. But the past year had humbled him and helped him to see that prayer changes things; and the more people praying the better. "Here's the thing, Erica. I lost my church almost a year ago because of the multiple affairs I've had." Erica didn't look shocked or like she was condemning him straight to hell for his failings, so he continued. "I have three children, but only two of them belong to my wife. Cassandra and I are trying to get full custody of my newest child.

"Even though I have repented and turned my life back to God, my wife still feels the pain of my adultery. She lives with it every day, and I want her to be free from it. Can you please pray that Cassandra will learn to trust me again?"

"I will," Erica said, then she punched JT on the shoulder and pointed in his face. "And you, you big jerk. Don't ever hurt her like that again."

That was the Erica he knew from high school; straightforward and to the point. JT lifted his arms in surrender. "You don't have to worry about me. I've learned the hard way. I've only loved two women in my life; you and Cassandra. I let you get away, but I don't ever want Cassandra to leave me. I don't know what I'd do if that happened."

Erica looked at her watch. "I've got to get back to work, but I will pray for Cassandra. Don't worry about that." She stood up and took her tray to the trash can before leaving the cafeteria.

Remembering that he had a message, JT picked his cell phone back up, opened it, and clicked on the message. It was picture mail. JT rolled his eyes as he wondered about the people who spent their day picture mailing folks. He normally deleted picture mail so fast that it didn't have time to register with Sprint that he'd received such a thing. But for some reason, JT couldn't make himself hit the delete button. He'd seen this cell number pop up on his phone before, he was sure of it. But he'd obviously not talked to the person enough to remember whose number it was. Curiosity got the better of him, and he opened the picture mail.

For a moment, JT thought his eyes were playing tricks on him. The woman in the photo looked like Cassandra, but she was holding hands with a man that JT didn't know. That couldn't be his wife... could it?

He dialed Cassandra's cell phone, and of course, it went straight to voice mail again. This time JT left a message. "Cassandra, I need to talk to you. Call me back as soon as you get my message." His tone was demanding, but at the moment JT didn't care.

He hung up and dialed his house. His evil mother-in-law picked up the phone again. JT got right to the point. "Put my wife on the phone now!"

"And just who do you think you're talking to?" Mattie said.

JT could picture hands on hips and the neck roll that he was sure was being displayed on the other end of the phone. So he gave back just as much attitude as he was getting. "I don't want to talk to you at all. I want you to stop answering my telephone or do as I say and get Cassandra to the phone this minute."

"Boy, I don't know what woman you are out of town with that has given you the courage to call here talking crazy. But Cassandra ain't here, and if she was, I wouldn't put her on the phone to take abuse from you," Mattie informed him, and then hung up in his face as usual.

JT shut his eyes as he hit the END button on his cell phone. He couldn't deal with this. He knew from deep within his heart that although he had done his wife wrong multiple times, he wouldn't be able to take her cheating on him. He looked to heaven and asked, "Why is this happening to us now, Lord?"

He could have understood if Cassandra had cheated on him while he was disrespecting and cheating on her. He wouldn't have been able to deal with that fact then either, but he would have understood why she would do such a thing. But *now*, when he was trying to be a better man? When he was struggling through her panic attacks and no sexual relations with his wife . . . Why would she do this to him now?

His eyes misted with tears as he thought about losing his first daughter and how that had torn him away from God. JT had promised God that nothing would ever separate him from His love again. But this . . . If God allowed Cassandra to cheat on him while he was trying to do the right thing, JT didn't know how he would recover from something like this.

Cassandra found two dresses and a pair of slacks that she really liked at the mall. She and JT had agreed not to spend any money outside of paying bills for the next two months. But JT would just have to deal with it. She was still smarting from that comment Diane made about calling JT's cell phone. Cassandra had decided not to go off the deep end until JT came home and was able to explain the situation to her. She was willing to give him the benefit of the doubt since she figured out that it had been Diane playing on her phone last night and not some other woman JT had started fooling around with. But that benefit was only going so far. If he had been talking to Diane behind her back, Cassandra was prepared to move out.

When she got home, she went straight upstairs and put her purchases on her bed, and then found her cell phone charger and plugged it into her cell phone. She went back downstairs and found her mother and all three children in the family room. Jerome and Aaron said "Hi" to her as she walked into the family room, then continued watching cartoons. Lily was in the playpen, and as soon as she saw Cassandra she started crying and holding her hands out, begging to be picked up. Cassandra gave her mother a knowing look. Lily had probably been left in the playpen the entire time, receiving none of the attention that Jerome and Aaron had received from their loving grandmother.

"Hey, sweetie," Cassandra said as she picked her up. She bounced her around and gave her a big hug, and then kissed her on the cheek, hoping that would make up for the affection she hadn't received this afternoon. She sat down with Lily on her lap and said, "Sorry, I took so long. I had this urge to buy something at the mall. I would have called, but my cell was dead."

"So that's why?" Mattie said, more to herself than to Cassandra.

"That's why what?"

"Oh, nothing. Did you find something pretty while you were out?" Mattie asked.

Cassandra smiled. "I sure did. I'm ready to kiss winter good-bye, so I purchased two spring dresses. JT is going to be mad because we're not supposed to spend any money for the next two months, but he'll get over it."

"Girl, I don't know how you put up with that broke man. I mean, when the boy had money, I could at least tell folks that you didn't care nothing about that flem-flam man. I told them that you were a gold digger."

"Mother!"

"Well, I did. Now what can I say? I'm stuck for the reason my daughter is stupid enough to stay married to such a . . . a—"

"Once again, I must remind you that you're saying this stuff in front of my children. Could you please stop?"

Mattie rolled her eyes as she said, "Y'all got too many rules in this house. Don't want nobody truth talking, so I'm just gon' shut up." She put her fingers to her mouth and acted as if she had a key and was locking her lips.

"You are such a drama queen," Cassandra said while shaking her head. "Anyway, did anybody call while I was gone?"

Mattie looked at Cassandra but didn't respond.

"Mother, did anybody call me?"

Again, Mattie did not respond.

Cassandra got up from the couch and took Lily upstairs with her. She turned her phone on so that she could check her messages while it was charging. That's when she noticed that JT had called her five times already. She listened to the messages and could tell that he was angry. His last message even accused her of avoiding his calls. When she finished listening to all five of JT's messages she hit END on her cell phone and started to dial his phone, but then realization struck her.

Diane must have sent that photo of her and Dr. Clarkson to JT. Cassandra stood up and paced around the room. Could her husband really believe that she was cheating on him? What was she supposed to do? Call JT back and tell him that she's not cheating, but seeing a therapist? She was uncomfortable about going to a therapist anyway, and she never wanted anyone to know that she had to talk to someone other than God about her issues.

She couldn't just let JT think she was a cheater, could she? Cassandra paced back and forth as she decided her course of action. What she really wanted to do was to go find Diane and beat some sense into that woman. Hadn't she done enough to her when she slept with her husband and had a baby by him? Did Cassandra really have to deal with this woman spying on her as well?

Ten

"Why haven't you returned any of my calls?" JT asked on Friday morning when Cassandra finally answered the telephone.

"Hello, JT, thanks for asking, I'm doing well. How about you?"

"This is no time to be cute, Cassandra. We need to talk."

"If talking to me was so important, you'd be home by now. But you're not, are you. Probably not even down there with Lamont. Probably got some woman in New Orleans."

"That's not even funny, Cassandra. But I know you've been in the house for days now with your mother, so it's no telling what she's filled your head with."

As soon as she said it, she wanted to take those words back. She knew how important it was to JT to help Lamont get his life together. And to find out that the boy had been hanging onto life by a thread had to be devastating to JT. "I'm sorry about that. How is Lamont doing?"

JT's smile could be heard through the phone as he said, "The doctors say that he's out of the woods. He looks a lot better too, Cassandra. And above all of that, he's finally agreed to come to Cleveland with me. I've been trying to call you to tell you that."

Now she felt bad for ignoring his calls. She'd thought that he wanted to talk with her about the pictures Diane took of her and Dr. Clarkson on Wednesday. And all this time, he'd just wanted to share his good news. "I got your messages, but my cell phone died on me. By the time I got it charged, the kids needed dinner, and then their baths, and time just got away from me."

"I understand. But why didn't you call me back yesterday. I left you messages on Thursday also."

"I didn't even check my messages yesterday, JT." That was true. She knew that JT had called seven times, because she was either in the room while her cell was ringing and didn't answer it, or she'd seen that she received a missed call from him. But not once yesterday did she check her voice mail. "Anyway," she said, changing the subject, "I'm glad Lamont has changed his mind about moving here."

"Yeah, me too." There was silence on the line and then JT asked, "How are the kids doing?"

"They're doing good. Driving me up a wall as usual."

Again, an uncomfortable silence on the line, and then JT said, "We need to talk, Cassandra. My flight leaves in an hour. Can you make sure that your mother is not there when I get home?"

"Are you planning to tell me about all the phone calls that Diane Benson has been making to your cell phone?" Cassandra said defiantly. Now she knew for sure that JT had received those pictures from Diane, but she wasn't going to let them make her feel bad. They were the ones that needed to answer for their actions.

"Diane called on Tuesday. She asked me to give Lily back to her. I told her that wasn't going to happen."

"Why didn't you tell me that you talked to her? How am I supposed to trust you if you hide things from me?" Cassandra demanded.

"I didn't have a chance. I got the phone call about Lamont before you got home and hadn't given Diane another thought."

"Mmh."

"It's the truth, Cassandra. I've been trying to show you for months now that I can be trusted. I do understand why it's taking you awhile to see that I've changed, but can we at least be reasonable with each other?"

Cassandra held the phone, but didn't respond. She knew that she hadn't been acting like a rational person of late, but what did he want from her? She was trying to get over his betrayal and the hurt it had caused. Some days were just harder than others.

"We're getting off the subject," JT said. "I need to ask you about a picture I received—"

"Ask me when you get home," Cassandra said testily, and then hung up the phone. She stood there for a moment with her hand on the receiver. She should call JT back. Cassandra wasn't sure why she had responded that way to him. Why didn't she just let him ask her about the picture so she could tell him who the guy was? She took her hand off the phone and turned to go check on the kids.

"Trouble in paradise?" Mattie asked when Cassandra turned around.

"Were you standing there listening to my conversation?"

"It's not like you're in the bedroom and I had my ear up against the door. You're standing right here in the living room."

"There is such a thing called common courtesy," Cassandra said as she rolled her eyes and tried to walk away from her mother.

"Don't you get snippy with me just because that husband

of yours is out catin' around. I didn't do this to you. I tried to warn you. I said, 'Don't marry him, Cassandra. He's going to unload a world of misery on you.'"

Cassandra rolled her eyes as she walked into the family room and sat down.

Mattie followed. "Every time I think about you and JT it reminds me of this joke I heard a TV preacher tell.

Cassandra groaned and buried her head in her hands.

Mattie continued, unfazed by her daughter's lack of interest. "It went like this . . . The devil interrupted this church service when he stood behind the pulpit and glared at the congregation.

"The congregation went wild. Everybody jumped out of their seats and fled the church. Everyone except for one lady who remained in her seat, looking toward the pulpit as if nothing out of the ordinary had just occurred.

"The devil looked at the woman and said, 'Everyone else has fled, aren't you afraid of me too?'

"She smirked as she continued to stare at him, 'Why should I be afraid? I've been married to your son for thirty years.'"

Cassandra stood up and faced off with her mother. "That's it. I am having enough trouble in my marriage without help from you."

"It's not my fault that you married that devil."

"JT is not the devil. He is trying to be a better man. Anyone with eyes can see that."

Mattie harrumphed as she said, "I don't know what kind of vision you got, Cassandra Ann. But I see a snake and a devil every time I look at your husband."

Maybe that was the problem. Cassandra could see now that her mother didn't want JT to change, so she would never see the truth. She would never see the man that JT Thomas had become . . . A loving, affectionate family man. But Cassandra saw the difference. She had lived with the man for eight years. She knew when JT was on the right path with the Lord, and had prayed everyday for his deliverance when he'd gone all wrong.

Nobody could tell her a thing about her husband that she didn't already know. She was married to a good man, and the only time she didn't believe it was when she was listening to her mother. "You've got to go," Cassandra said with finality in her voice.

"So you're throwing me out of your house again, huh?"

Cassandra knew her mother was referring to the time when JT got so fed up with her put downs that he told her to get out of their house, and Cassandra didn't stop him. She had felt guilty about allowing her mother to be thrown out of her home that day. But her mother was a bitter and unhappy woman, and Cassandra couldn't be around her right now. "I'm sorry, Mother. But this is the way it has to be. Until you can respect my husband, you can't be around the children anymore either."

"What?" Mattie exploded. "I love my grandchildren, and they love me. You are wrong for this, Cassandra."

"How many grandchildren do you have, Mother?"

"I have two, Jerome and Aaron," Mattie answered without a moment's hesitation.

"That's the problem," Cassandra told her. "Because I have three children. Lily has become just as much a part of me as Jerome and Aaron. And I won't let you mistreat her anymore."

"You cannot take my grandchildren away from me," Mattie screamed.

"I don't want to, Mother. But the things you say about

their father around them are not helpful at all. I can't allow that anymore." Somebody must be praying for her strength, Cassandra thought. Because she didn't even know where all of this 'truth talking' as her mother called it, was coming from. She normally allowed her mother to get away with saying just about anything, thinking that if she ignored her, she would stop. But something inside of her clicked when she hung up the phone with JT. It was as if God Himself allowed her to see that she wasn't giving him a fair shake. Cassandra knew one thing for sure right now – she wanted her marriage to work. And if that's what she wanted, she would have to stop spending so much time rehashing the past. "I'm going to pray for you, Mother. You've got too much bitterness locked inside you right now. You can't see it, but watching you carry that bitterness around is draining me of all the strength I have."

"Oh, so I'm a bitter old woman, am I?" Mattie opened the closet, grabbed her overnight bag and her purse. She then went up the stairs and into Jerome and Aaron's room. She kissed them while they slept. As she came out of the room she angrily turned her back to Lily's door and marched back down the stairs. "This bitter old woman knows how to leave a place where she's not wanted." She opened the front door, and then turned back to glare at Cassandra. "You just remember this, girl. I changed your diapers and put food in your belly. I put a roof over your head and gave your children a place to stay when you left that no good husband that you're standing there protecting." She pointed at her as she said, "You're not going to keep my grandchildren away from me."

As Mattie slammed the door, Cassandra sat down on the bottom step in the entryway and cried. She loved JT and she loved her mother. Why did the two of them always force her to choose?

***

Fuming from ear to ear, Mattie cursed like a sailor as she drove home. She hadn't asked to come over to their raggedy old house. Cassandra had called and asked her to spend a few nights with her. If she was that bad of a person, why would Cassandra want to spend time with her in the first place?

First JT took the kids away from her on Tuesday, and now her own daughter had the audacity to say that she wasn't welcomed there and that she couldn't see her grandchildren, like she was poison or something. Did they think she would infect the kids with words? Or were they just afraid to hear the truth?

"Cassandra has turned her back on me one too many times. And for a baby that's not even hers," Mattie fussed as she turned into her driveway.

She parked the car, got out and stomped all the way to her front door. When she opened the door an odor caught her attention and she rushed into the kitchen to find that she had forgotten to take the trash out. Now she was really mad with Cassandra. Trying to do something for that ungrateful girl, she'd left all this stanking trash in her house, and now she was going to need to deodorize the place. She grabbed the trash bag and walked it to the trash can outside.

When she came back in the house she noticed that the light was flashing on her answering machine. She walked over to it and pushed the button to listen to her messages. The box told her that she had five awaiting messages. The first, second, and third messages were from bill collectors. Didn't they know she was retired and on a fixed income? She had been working part-time at a local dress shop. But when so many people started losing their homes to foreclosure, the business at the dress shop dried up. Guess people didn't care about looking good when they were living out of their cars.

The next call was from nosey old Sister Ellen at the church she had been attending. "Hey, Sister Mattie, I was just checking on you. We haven't seen you at church in a few Sundays, and the Senior Saints missed you at our outing last weekend. I'd sure like to hear from you. Well, I'll be praying for your strength in the Lord."

"Pray on, Sister Ellen, pray on," Mattie said as she deleted the call. She was sick of attending church and making nice with all them hypocrites. The only reason she joined that church in the first place was because Cassandra wanted to be in a house of worship while she and JT were separated. Once she went back home to him, she started attended his little broke down church.

When the next message played, Mattie had to sit down and take it in. Maybe there was a God and He was finally giving her a reason to keep on living. Diane Benson's voice boomed through her answering machine. "Miss Mattie, I know you don't like me. But you need to know that what happened with me and JT is over and done with. I just want my daughter back, and I was hoping that you might be willing to help me." Diane left her telephone number, and then said, "I have a plan, but I'm going to need your help to make it work."

A smile crept across Mattie's face. She would walk a mile on nails, swim from Cleveland to Timbuktu if it meant getting Lily out of Cassandra's house. Yes, she would help Diane with whatever plan she had concocted. Cassandra would be mad at first, but she would come to understand that she shouldn't be raising some other woman's child. She had plenty enough on her hands raising them two boys and that good-for-nothing husband of hers.

Eleven

JT was angry when Cassandra hung up the phone in his face. That had clenched it for him. He knew from experience how to evade and avoid questions, and that was what Cassandra was doing now. If she weren't guilty and didn't have anything to hide, she wouldn't have been avoiding him all week.

Facing the facts, he told himself that his wife was cheating on him. It wasn't in his wife's nature to be with more than one man at a time. That was one of the reasons he'd married her. After catching his first wife in bed with another man, JT had wanted a woman who would be true to him. For eight years, Cassandra had been that woman. Why would she throw what they had away after everything they had already been through?

Cassandra wasn't having panic attacks when he touched her because she couldn't stop thinking about JT's unfaithful past. She was having those attacks because she didn't want to be touched by anyone but her new lover. Now he knew the god awful truth and it hurt even more than when his first wife had betrayed him.

JT had never loved Mona. He'd married her because he thought she had been pregnant with his child. But that proved to be a lie. So when he found her in bed with another man; that became JT's one-way ticket out of a bad marriage. He'd never looked back. But this was Cassandra. The mother of his children and the love he had waited a lifetime for. Could he walk away from her without looking back?

"What's eating at you?" Lamont asked as JT walked back in the hospital room with him.

"What are you talking about?" JT asked while putting his cell phone back on his hip clamp.

"You look like your woman just ran off with the mailman."

JT tried to laugh, but it sounded forced. He jokingly said, "My kids run my wife in too many circles for her to have time to say more than three words to our mailman." JT bent down and picked up his duffel bag. He turned back to Lamont. "My flight leaves in a couple of hours."

A sorrowful expression appeared in Lamont's eyes. JT wanted to hug the boy, just as if he were his very own son. They had come a long way from the day Lamont blew him off in that restaurant.

"Now what are you looking all sad for? You don't even have a wife, so no mailman stole her away from you."

"I think I'm going to miss you hanging around here," Lamont said honestly.

JT pointed a finger at him. "You just remember your promise. The minute you finish the rehab for your arm, you're going to get on a plane and come stay with me and Cassandra."

Lamont nodded. "You've got my word on that. This accident convinced me that I need to change my life. I also figured that I needed to start hanging around a better class of people."

"Amen to that." JT walked closer to Lamont, shook his good hand, and then said, "I'm glad I met you. You're a good guy."

"All right, all right, enough with all this touchy feely stuff. Get on home to your wife before she forgets what you look like."

Another toneless laugh escaped JT's mouth as he walked out of the room. In truth, JT was sick at the thought that another man might just have wiped his memory out of Cassandra's heart. On the plane ride home, JT told himself over and over again that he wouldn't be able to deal with Cassandra cheating on him. He'd left Mona the minute he discovered her cheating ways and JT feared he would do the same if Cassandra confirmed his suspicions. Men were built different than women. JT had had sleepless nights ever since he opened that god awful picture mail. Every time he tried to close his eyes he would picture Cassandra in another man's arms.

Now he knew for sure the awful pain of rejections and uncertainty that he'd put his wife through with his unfaithful actions. He would buy her a thousand roses, pluck the petals off of each one and lay them at her feet to thank her for taking him back. After going through the agony of betrayal he'd endured this week, he honestly didn't know how Cassandra had found it in her heart to forgive him.

But had she really forgiven him? Wasn't that why she had those panic attacks when he tried to touch her? Maybe Cassandra couldn't forgive either. Maybe that's why she took up with this other guy . . . to forget the pain and misery he'd brought her.

When he got off the plane, he walked toward the baggage area like a man on death row, walking his last mile. His heart was so heavy, he'd almost convinced himself that he didn't want to know the truth. He wouldn't ask Cassandra anything when he got home, they'd just go on living the way they had been. But he knew he couldn't do that. His pride wouldn't allow him to live like that.

JT then realized that the prideful part of him had been

whispering in his ear ever since he saw that picture of Cassandra. Hadn't Cassandra relinquished her pride when she took him back?

He picked up his bag and turned to go get his car out of the long term parking lot as an older couple caught his attention. They didn't look ageless or beautiful. They looked tired and worn out, like they had weathered many a storm, but the way they held hands and smiled at one another told JT they had been victorious. And now as they entered the twilight of their lives, they were at peace with each other.

It was at that moment that JT decided his pride would not cost him a lifetime with the woman he loved. He would grow old and wrinkly with Cassandra even if he had to forgive her for infidelity. Maybe he would have a few panic attacks like Cassandra had been doing lately, but they'd get through that as well. With renewed vigor, JT headed toward his car. His mind was set. He was going home to fight for his marriage.

Cassandra had taken to her bed with weeping and moaning. She was miserable and she couldn't even call Dr. Clarkson for an appointment for fear that Diane would be lurking someplace, trying to take another picture of them. Everything was going wrong. Her mother was mad at her, JT was mad at her. But on the other hand, she was mad at her mother and she was mad at JT also. It was a vicious circle that was taking her 'round and 'round, and Cassandra didn't know how to stop the ride and get off.

She continued to weep silently into her pillow as she curled up in a ball on her bed. The night Diane did her heavy breathing on her telephone, Cassandra had figured out what the problem was. She was so bound up with fear that JT would break her heart again that she couldn't move forward.

Cassandra wanted her marriage to work, but how could it when she was so afraid all the time? The minute JT walked out the door, she found herself wondering if he would meet someone and have another affair. If he were late getting home, or didn't answer her call, she imagined all types of illicit activity were going on. She was tired of it and knew she couldn't live like this much longer, but she had no one to turn to, and didn't know who could help her. And then for no particular reason at all, in between sobs, Cassandra began to hum the words to a Mary Mary song. She hummed and cried, hummed and cried until she got to the part that said, *Maybe you're confused about who I really am . . . I'm God.*

Cassandra sat up and lifted her head as though she was looking at heaven and began to pray. "Is that it, Lord? Am I going through all this misery because I've been trying to lean on everyone but you? Please help me, Lord. What do I need to do?"

She continued to sit in the spot she was in, hoping that none of the children would wake up kicking and screaming as they normally did. Right now she wanted the Lord to have her undivided attention. "I want to love JT. But he broke my heart, and I'm so afraid that he'll do it again."

Trust. She heard the Lord speak that word into her heart.

A smile began to creep across Cassandra's face. "So are you saying that if I trust JT, I will be able to give him my heart?"

No answer came, but a peace began to wash over her at the thought of trusting JT with her heart. And if this would result in letting go of the fear she carried around with her day in and day out, then so much the better. She got off the bed and found that Mary Mary CD she was just thinking about. JT had bought her that CD a couple of weeks ago, and she'd listened to it so much that it seemed as if it were finally sinking in. She turned the first song on. The words "*I'm a believer*" shouted through the speakers as Mary Mary sang the words of Cassandra's heart. She danced all around her room, enjoying the Lord.

Jerome burst open her bedroom door. He stood there for a moment with a puzzled look on his face and then asked, "Wha 'cha doing?"

"I'm praise dancing, baby. Come join me." Cassandra grabbed Jerome's hands and spun him around.

He laughed. "Do it again, Mommy."

Cassandra picked him up and danced across the room with her little man. She and Jerome were in such high spirits as they laughed and danced that they didn't hear the front door open. Nor did they hear the foot steps on the stairs. Cassandra swirled around with Jerome and almost dropped him when she saw JT leaned against the doorpost watching them.

JT rushed over to help hold Jerome in her arms so he wouldn't fall. Jerome appeared oblivious to the fact that he'd almost landed on the floor. "Dance with us, Daddy," he shouted.

"You two are in good spirits," JT said as he moved to the music with them. They danced around the room, and then Jerome wanted to be put down.

As soon as Jerome was on his own two feet, he danced his way out of their room. Nervous to be left alone with JT, Cassandra asked Jerome, "Where are you going?"

"To get a toy," he said as he kept dancing down the hall.

Cassandra tried to follow behind her son, but JT put his hand on her arm halting her. "Where's your mother?"

"I sent her home," Cassandra told him.

"Why'd you send her home?"

She didn't look at him, too ashamed of her hard headedness. "You were right, JT. My mother is just too bitter right now to be around the kids."

JT hugged her. "Thank you, Cassandra," he said, and then as he pulled away he asked, "Can I talk to you for a minute?"

His eyes were so full of love for her. She wanted to just lean in and let the loving begin, but so much had happened, and she and JT still had so much to iron out. She didn't blame JT though. Cassandra was beginning to think that she had moved back in with him too soon. She hadn't healed from all the pain he'd caused her. Funny thing was, at this moment, she wanted to be healed. She wanted to just let go and let God work this out for her.

She could do this. The Lord would help her. She nodded, getting ready to say okay, but then Lily woke, screaming and crying and Aaron followed suit. She turned toward the door and said, "Let's talk tonight. I need to see about these kids, okay?"

JT followed behind her. He went into Aaron's room and picked him up while Cassandra picked up Lily. They all went downstairs and into the family room. Cassandra put Lily in the playpen, and then went into the kitchen to warm up dinner.

JT walked up behind her and turned her around. He lifted her chin so that she was looking into his eyes. "You've been crying," he said.

"Yes," she answered honestly. "But let's talk about it tonight.

Twelve

They were in their bedroom. Cassandra was seated on the stool in front of her vanity and JT had just stepped out of the shower. He had on loose fitting, cotton pajama pants and a T-shirt. He saw Cassandra watching him, and he hoped that look in her eyes meant what he thought. But he had to get something straight before he could even go there.

Thankfully though, Cassandra put him out of his misery before he even asked the question. "Look, JT, I know you received a picture of me with another man either on your cell phone or through e-mail."

"How do you know that?"

"Because I saw Diane take the pictures, and she told me that she was going to send it to you."

JT snapped his fingers together. "I knew that picture was sent to me from a number I should have recognized. But then she checks on her child so little, I didn't remember her number."

"According to Diane, she talks to you quite frequently. She even dared me to check the cell phone bill to find out just how much she calls you."

"That's a lie. The first time I talked to that woman in months was Tuesday when she called to tell me she was back in town and wanted Lily."

"So you don't mind if I check the cell phone bill?"

"Absolutely not. Feel free to check it," he said like a man with nothing to hide. "Now do you mind telling me who this man in the picture is?"

Cassandra stood up. She hesitated long enough for JT's knees to give out. He sat on the edge of the bed and looked at her again. She was everything he wanted. He wished he'd known that simple fact years ago when he was uselessly playing the field. He would give anything if he could take back the hurt he'd caused her. But maybe there was something he could do. He could accept her with her flaws, just as she had done for him. As Cassandra finally opened her mouth to speak, JT lifted his hand. "Forget it. I don't want to know. Just tell me one thing."

"What's that?"

"Are you planning to leave me?"

"If you had asked me that question earlier this week or even earlier today, I wouldn't have been able to give you an answer. My mind has been in so much turmoil that I haven't been able to think clearly."

"Are . . . you . . . in . . . love . . . with . . . him?" Every word that escaped JT's mouth caused a slow death to his heart. He held his breath, waiting on an answer.

Cassandra rushed over to JT as she shook her head. "Oh no. You've got it all wrong. I'm not seeing anyone else. The turmoil I've been going through has nothing to do with another man."

"But what about the picture, Cassandra? You were holding that man's hand."

"No I wasn't. If anything, he was holding my hand. And I'm still not sure why he grabbed my hand when he did." She sat down on the bed next to JT and put his hand in hers. "I was wrong for not answering your phone calls this week, I knew what you wanted. I just wasn't ready to tell you what was really going on."

He liked that she was holding his hand, but he was still hesitant when he asked, "And what has been going on."

"I felt so bad about the panic attacks I've been having and the fact that I didn't know what was causing them that I started seeing a therapist. Every Tuesday when you take the kids, I go to see Dr. Clarkson."

"But that picture wasn't taken on Tuesday was it?"

"No. I had another panic attack on Tuesday night, so I called Dr. Clarkson and asked if I could meet with him. He was nice enough to meet me for lunch; we just didn't know that Diane would be filming us." Cassandra shook her head as she remembered Diane's hateful words.

It was as if JT didn't hear anything about Diane filming his wife. His mind was strictly focused on one thing. "I still don't understand why this so-called therapist held onto your hand like he did."

"It's really not the big deal you're trying to make it. It was nothing. I don't even remember what we were talking about when he grabbed my hand. All I know is that Diane was Johnny-on-the-spot with snapping that picture, because I pulled my hand out of his as soon as he grabbed it."

JT stood up and paced the room. "I don't think you should go to this therapist anymore. I don't trust him. Mark my words, Cassandra. He's up to something."

"If you would just sit back down and listen to me, I'm trying to tell you that I don't think I need to see Dr. Clarkson anymore anyway."

He whirled around to face his wife. "What do you mean? What else happened?"

"I finally figured out that all this fear and anxiety I've been going through is a direct result of my not trusting you. Right before you came home, I handed all my problems over to God. I'm done stressing."

"Why did you have a panic attack on Tuesday night? You've normally had those when... you know; when I touch you."

"That's what I'm trying to tell you. It had nothing to do with your touch, but everything to do with my fear of you not being true. On Tuesday evening, someone called here breathing heavy into the phone, I figured out it was Diane the next day. But that night, my mother convinced me that it was some new woman of yours playing on the phone and I spazed out."

"You're the only woman I want, Cassandra. If I didn't know that before, I certainly figured it out this week."

Cassandra stood back up, she didn't move away from JT though. "I want to believe that, JT. It's just that we've been through so much that sometimes it's hard for me to accept that you truly want me. But I decided something when I was in this room crying my eyes out earlier." She sat back down and looked him directly in the eye as she said, "I'm tired of crying and stressing over you, JT. I'm either going to trust you, or pack my bags and leave."

"I need you to trust me, baby. I don't ever want you to leave me again."

"Then I need your help, JT. I've decided to give you my heart, but I need you to be more than a man... I need you to be God's man."

He raised his hand to her face and gently stroked it. When she didn't recoil at his touch, he silently prayed that her words were true and that his wife had finally come back to him. "You've got a deal, baby," he said as he covered her mouth with his.

Cassandra didn't move away. She squeezed in closer and

enjoyed the moment. When he came up for air, she asked, "So what do we do now?"

JT laughed. "See, woman, it's been so long, you've forgotten what to do." He picked her up and gently placed her in the middle of the bed. He turned out the lights and they trusted each other with their love all night long.

Thirteen

The rest of the weekend was magical for JT. His wife had finally let go of her fears and fallen back into his arms. They spent all day Saturday feeding the kids and rushing them back to their rooms for a nap. Their children took so many naps on Saturday that they were sluggish on Sunday morning and kept nodding off as JT preached to his small congregation. JT tried not to take it personally that his children couldn't keep their eyes open during his sermons. Before he could get too discouraged he noticed that two new faces were seated amongst his regulars.

Cassandra noticed them also and rushed to them after service. She shook the couple's hands and said, "Welcome. I hope you enjoyed the service."

"We did," the woman told Cassandra, and then added, "I was just telling my husband that we should come back next Sunday."

"Oh, you have to come back. JT is one of the most anointed pastor's in this city. I guarantee you'll get something out of his messages," Cassandra gushed.

"Don't mind her, she's my wife, so she sees me through the eyes of love," JT said as he joined the group and put his arm around Cassandra's waist. The woman his wife was talking to was Halle Berry beautiful, but as far as JT was concerned, Cassandra lit up his world and caused him to see only her.

"Shush, boy, even if I wasn't your wife, I'd tell people what an anointed man of God you are."

Beaming from ear to ear, JT shook hands with the couple in front of them. "I guess you know that I'm Pastor JT Thomas."

The man smiled also as he said, "Kind of hard to miss that. I'm Eric Peoples, and this is my wife, Ellen."

JT turned to Cassandra and asked, "Did you already introduce yourself, honey?"

"I was just getting to that when you interrupted us with all that false humility," she said jokingly. "I'm Cassandra Thomas. I meant what I said before; I hope the two of you decide to come back again."

JT hugged Cassandra. "Yes, please come back, and invite friends if you like. We need to start filling up these empty seats."

"The way you preach, I don't think these seats are going to be empty for long," Ellen told JT.

JT thought he noticed something in the woman's eyes as she spoke to him, but then he shook his suspicions off. Coming from his past history with women in the church, he was naturally a little suspicious of people, but that didn't mean everyone had an ulterior motive just because he had once had ulterior motives for most things he did. "Well, hopefully we'll see you guys next Sunday. But right now I need to take my wife and kids home," JT told them as he and Cassandra walked away.

"Why'd you brush them off like that?" Cassandra asked when she, JT, and the kids were in his car and headed home. "We're trying to rebuild our church. We can't afford to be acting like we're too busy to chat."

"Look at you." JT was grinning as he drove home. "I've

never seen you so interested in growing our church membership before."

"When you started pastoring at Faith Outreach, they had
at least about three hundred members. Now we have less than
thirty. In case you haven't noticed, brother-man, you've got
three kids and a wife to feed. So you need a few hundred or
so more tithe paying members before you can go back into
full-time ministry."

"Who said I was thinking about giving up my job?"

"I know you, JT. Your ministry is the church, and you
won't rest until you are a full-time pastor. But, like I said, your
family needs to eat."

JT laughed. "Okay, okay. I'll take out more time for new
people," he said, but then an idea struck him. "Why don't
you handle our church growth program?"

"Me?"

"Yeah, you. The one that likes to eat."

Cassandra elbowed JT for that crack, but then asked, "Do
you really think I can help?"

One of the problems JT and Cassandra had early on in his
ministry was that Cassandra didn't feel needed. There were
tons of people ready to do whatever JT wanted, and he'd
looked over his wife in favor of the elders, deacons, and min-
isters. But now he needed her, and he was going to make
sure she knew it. "The way you pounced on those new people
today, I'm positive you can develop a program that will help
us grow our membership in no time."

She pointed her index finger at JT. "I didn't pounce, but
I'll take that as a compliment anyway."

Once they were home and settled in, JT again suggested
that the kids needed a nap.

Jerome protested this time. "Ah-uh, no way, I'm all napped
out, Daddy."

JT looked to Cassandra for help, but she was too busy giggling. He turned back to his eldest son and said, "Boy, if you don't get yourself up them stairs, I'ma have a fit on you."

Jerome grabbed his toy men and started running toward the stairs. Cassandra got up and ran after him. "Jerome, slow down. Come back here." She grabbed him and turned him back around.

Jerome screamed, "No Mommy, I don't want Daddy to have a fit on me."

"You don't even know what that means, and your daddy is not going to have a fit on you," Cassandra assured her son.

"Yes I am," JT said in a playful manner. He's interrupting my private time with my wife."

"Well, your wife needs some family time."

JT stuck his chest out like the big man on campus. "Oh, I'm not enough family for you?"

"Not at the moment, sir. Right now I'd like to see about my children if you don't mind."

Dejected, JT sat down and turned the television on. "All right the kids win this round. What do you want to watch, Jerome?"

"*Blues Clues*," Jerome said as he excitedly jumped around in his mother's arms.

Cassandra put Jerome down as she whispered in his ear. "Go give your daddy a hug for not throwing a fit."

"Okay," Jerome said as he ran toward his dad and wrapped his short arms around him. "Thank you for not being mad, Daddy."

"Thank you for that wonderful hug, son," JT replied.

Jerome got on the couch and snuggled next to his father as he watched *Blues Clues* with a content expression on his boyish face.

Cassandra picked up her cell phone and snapped a picture of father and son. "Now that's a Hallmark moment," she said as she looked at them through eyes of love.

JT looked over at the playpen where Aaron and Lily lay sleeping contently. "You know what we need? A family photo."

"Yeah," Cassandra agreed. "We haven't had one since Aaron was two months. I'll make the arrangements." Cassandra sat down on the couch with her boys. They remained like that for another hour, until Jerome's head began to bob. JT laid him on the couch and then gave Cassandra a raised eyebrow.

Before she could respond, Lily woke up with a shout. "I guess that means, not now," she told him as she pulled Lily out of the playpen.

JT shook his head. "I'm going to have to do something about these treacherous kids."

They spent the evening with the children, enjoying their family, but when the lights went out it was all about JT and Cassandra. That was a truly happy night for them, which was a good thing; because the next night their world fell apart.

When JT arrived home from work on Monday evening, he walked into the kitchen, kissed the cook, and then kissed each one of his children.

"Aren't we in a good mood this evening," Cassandra said while stirring the spaghetti sauce.

"Why wouldn't I be in a good mood? I've got a lovely wife and three adorable, well behaved children."

"Hah," Cassandra said as she laughed. "You should have been here earlier and you would have seen just how well behaved your children are."

JT opened his mouth to respond, but the doorbell rang. "Let me get this door, and then I'll be back to defend my children."

"Whatever, you aren't in this house with them all day long. So you don't know how b-a-d your children are."

JT was smiling with his eyes and strutting with vigor as he looked through the peephole and saw Bishop Turner and Sam Unders standing on his front porch. He opened the door and gave both men a bear hug. "Hey, what brings you two out this evening?"

There was a grim expression on Bishop and Unders's faces as they stepped into the house. "Hey, JT," they both said in unison.

"What's with the long faces?" JT asked as he closed the door.

Drying her hands as she walked into the living room, Cassandra took one look at their guest and stopped. "What is it? What's wrong?"

With one look in Cassandra's direction, JT could tell that fear was trying to take hold of her again. He turned to Bishop and Unders and told them, "If y'all gon' be in my house, we need to see some smiles on your faces."

"How are you doing, Cassandra?" Bishop asked his daughter.

"I'm okay," she responded with as little enthusiasm as possible.

"I left you a message earlier this morning. I was hoping we could do lunch, but you didn't call me back," Bishop Turner said.

"I was busy with the kids." Cassandra didn't make eye contact with her father. She just stood there looking as if she wanted an escape from this conversation.

"I understand," Bishop said, and then turned back to JT. "Can we speak somewhere privately?"

"Privately? What's that supposed to mean . . . You don't want me there? Aren't you and JT tired of secrets?" Cassandra huffed, and then whirled around and went back into the kitchen.

The last thing JT wanted Cassandra to think was that he was keeping secrets from her. They had crossed a major milestone in their relationship this weekend, and he wanted them to continue progressing. He followed Cassandra into the kitchen. They were standing by the stove while the children sat around the kitchen table; Lily and Aaron were both in highchairs. JT whispered in Cassandra's ear, "I don't have any secrets."

"Then why does he want to talk in private?" she shot back.

"I don't know. But you are more than welcome to sit with us. Why don't you go tell them to have a seat and let me fix the kids' their plates."

Cassandra hesitated, but then she handed JT the towel she had been drying her hands on and headed toward the living room.

"All right, who wants spaghetti?" JT asked as he picked up the first plate.

"Me, me," Jerome and Aaron both yelled.

"Coming right up," JT said as he fixed the plates. He handed Jerome his, but chopped Lily and Aaron's food up. Aaron liked to feed himself, so JT only had to feed Lily. "I sure wish I had some food," he said to the kids as he watched them shovel it in.

Jerome laughed. "There's food in the pot, Daddy."

"Okay, I'll eat after me and your mommy take care of something," JT told Jerome.

"Ah man, do we have to take another nap?" Jerome complained.

"You sure do, young man. So hurry up and eat your food so you can go to sleep."

Cassandra walked back into the kitchen and told JT, "They want to know how much longer you're going to be."

JT was feeding Lily. He looked up at Cassandra and said, "I was thinking about putting them to bed before we talked with them."

Cassandra shook her head. "That's going to take too much time. They're going to fight us all the way. Just put them in the family room and turn on the television. We can sit in the kitchen and talk to them so that we can still see the kids."

"Beautiful and smart," JT said, trying to take the strained look off of Cassandra's face.

"Are you guys done?" Cassandra asked Jerome and Aaron without responding to JT's comment.

Both boys shook their heads. She grabbed a couple of wet wipes and wiped the excess spaghetti sauce off their faces and hands. "Go on in the family room. I'll be there in a minute," she said as she took Aaron out of his high chair. She then handed JT a wet wipe and told him to clean Lily up.

It took about ten minutes, but the children were comfortably in the family room watching cartoons. The kitchen table had been cleaned off, and now, JT and Cassandra sat at the table with Bishop and Unders. "Okay, gentlemen, "JT said, "let's have it. But please keep your voices down. My children are in the next room." Actually the house had an open floor plan from the kitchen to the family room, so the children were on the other side of the island.

Bishop cleared his throat, and then spoke in as low a tone as he could. "I hate to come over here with bad news, but you'll know about this soon enough, so I thought it would be good for us to strategize how we are going to handle this matter."

"What matter are you talking about?" Cassandra asked with a little sista-sista in her voice.

Bishop turned toward his daughter, he put his hand over hers, and Cassandra moved her hand away. "I'm trying to handle this as delicately as possible, Cassandra. I know that you've had to deal with an awful lot of late, and I don't want to cause you extra stress."

"Why? Do you think I'm a basket case, like my husband accused me of being last week?" Cassandra asked.

JT didn't know where all this was coming from. He and Cassandra had spent a wonderful weekend together, and he honestly thought they had moved past a lot of their issues. But she was acting as if nothing had changed between them. He wanted whatever it was out on the table already, so he and Cassandra could move back to where they had been before he opened the front door and let his friend and father-in-law in. "Can you just spit it out, sir? All this beating around the bush is getting Cassandra nervous."

With eyes on fire, Cassandra turned to JT and said, "Do I look nervous? I'm just tired of secrets and hushed conversations."

JT wanted to tell Cassandra that she did indeed look nervous, but that she had no reason to be because he hadn't done anything. Instead, he turned to Bishop and waited.

Clearing his throat again, Bishop said, "Diane Benson's attorney has served the church with a sexual abuse lawsuit."

Fourteen

"What?" JT exploded as he lifted himself out of his seat.

"She claims that you misused your position of authority in order to manipulate her into having a sexual relationship with you," Unders told him.

"She initiated the affair. I never manipulated that woman into anything," JT said as he lowered his voice.

"There's more," Bishop said. He kept his eyes averted from Cassandra as he continued. "Margie Milner's name has been added to the suit. She is also accusing you of manipulation."

JT sat back down and put his head in his hands. He'd had three affairs on his wife. Diane had approached him and he'd been only too willing to fall into her trap. But he had initiated the affairs with both Margie and Vivian Sampson. Vivian had already been crazy before he'd ever approached her, he just didn't know it. But Margie had been dedicated to the Lord. Now she was an unwed mother, living in sin. And he couldn't get around the fact that he was the reason. "So why didn't I receive the paperwork for this lawsuit? Why do you two know about it before me?"

Because Diane and Margie want five hundred thousand each, and they want it from the church," Unders told him.

"What?" JT exploded again.

"You heard me," Unders said.

Jerome ran into the kitchen and said, "Daddy, stop yelling. I can't hear the TV."

"Sorry, son," JT apologized. "I'll keep my voice down. You go on back in the family room."

When Jerome turned around to leave, Cassandra stood up from the table, and without saying word to JT or anyone else, she walked into the family room and sat down with her children.

"I'm sorry, JT," Bishop said as he watched Cassandra walk away. "Maybe we should have asked you to come to the church in the morning, but I have to fly out of here early in the morning."

JT waved that comment off. "She would have found out anyway. It's best that it's out in the open."

Bishop leaned over to JT and said, "She won't even talk to me. I know this whole situation is going to hurt her all over again. But I don't know what to do. How can I help her?"

"I wish I knew, Bishop. I thought we had made progress this weekend. But you saw how she just acted toward me. I'm in the dog house all over again, so I don't know what to do either."

"May I suggest that the two of you be patient with Cassandra? She's had to deal with a lot of changes in the space of a year, so she's going to need time to process how she feels about all of this," Elder Unders told them. JT had confided in Unders about everything he and his family had been dealing with.

"Yeah," JT whispered. "She's been seeing a therapist. So maybe he can help her deal with her issues."

Bishop turned to look at Cassandra as she held Aaron on her lap, with her back toward them. "I sure hope this therapist can help."

"When this is all over, I might need an appointment with him myself," JT said.

"Me too," said Unders.

"You know what I don't understand? Why would they sue the church when I'm no longer there?" JT asked.

"It's quite simple, my boy. The church has the money to pay and you don't," Bishop said while stretching out his legs underneath the table.

Cassandra wanted to walk back in that kitchen and do an unholy dance on her husband's head. Diane Benson was never going to leave them alone. She was a mean, hateful, and vindictive woman. JT had brought her into their lives, and at that moment, Cassandra didn't know if she would ever forgive him for that.

This lawsuit wasn't about the money to Diane. She didn't get Lily back when she'd finally decided that she wanted her, so now she was going to humiliate them instead. Diane would drag Cassandra's family through the mud. She could just see that evil woman on the Oprah show crying about how JT took advantage of her. And telling the entire world that his wife wasn't woman enough to keep him at home.

When Bishop came into the family room to say goodnight to her, Cassandra glanced at him and mumbled, "Night." She knew she was wrong. But Bishop had introduced her to JT; so the way Cassandra saw it, he was just as much to blame as JT for the misery she had to suffer through.

Aaron had fallen asleep, Lily was in her playpen quietly playing with her toys, and Jerome's eyes were glued to the TV. Bishop walked away from Cassandra and gave Jerome and Lily a hug, and then offered both of them a piece of candy.

"They can't have that," Cassandra said as she stood up and asked, "Are you ready to leave?"

"Yes, we were on our way out," Bishop said as he straightened up.

"Then let me walk you to the door," Cassandra said as she and JT walked their guests to the living room and let them out the front door. When they were alone, Cassandra turned to JT and said, "I need to talk to you." She climbed the steps to their bedroom without waiting for a response from him. As she entered the room, she saw JT's Bible on top of the dresser. She picked it up and threw it at him as he walked in behind her.

He caught his Bible and looked at her quizzically.

"What does God tell you to do for me?"

"Huh?"

She pointed at the Bible "That book in your hand, what does it say? It tells you to love your wife, right? Not love every and any other woman that you come in contact with."

He sat the Bible on the nightstand and turned back to his wife. "Cassandra, I know you're mad. And you have every right to be. You shouldn't have to deal with any of this, but here we are."

"No," Cassandra corrected him with her hands on her hips. "Here *you* are. I'm not about to let you drag this family through the mud like this. So you better fix this and fix it quick."

"What do you want me to do, Cassandra?"

"Settle it out of court."

"How? They want a million dollars."

"No. They want five hundred thousand a piece. Offer them a hundred thousand each and settle it."

"Even if they would take a hundred thousand, where would I get that kind of money? You've seen our bank account just as well as I have. We don't have it."

Cassandra's foot started tapping as she stared at JT like he was some slick used car salesman stringing together one lie after the other. "What about the hundred and twenty-five thousand in our savings account?"

Now it was JT's turn to look at Cassandra crazy. "You know that money belongs to Lamont. How can you even ask me to spend his money on something like this?"

"You didn't have a problem spending the money when it was supposed to go to Lamont's father. Back then you spent it on a house and a car and you are going to stand there and tell me that your wife and children aren't worth more than a house and a car?"

"That's not what I'm saying at all, Cassandra. But a man should pay his debts. I owed Jimmy that money and he asked me to give it to his son and that's what I intend to do."

"What about the debt you owe your family?"

"I owe you all my loyalty, my commitment, and my love." He walked toward her and attempted to put his arms around her as he said, "But that money isn't ours. I won't steal from Lamont."

She pushed him away from her as she glared at him.

"I need you to be with me on this one, Cassandra."

She walked over to the bed, pulled the blanket off, and threw it at JT. "And I need you to sleep downstairs."

"Cassandra, be reasonable."

"I've been too reasonable. That's the problem." She picked up a glass and threw it at his head.

JT ducked and the glass shattered against the bedroom door. JT's eyes bucked. "Cassandra!" he said as if he were shocked at her behavior.

She walked over to the mantle to grab hold of the glass picture frame that held their wedding photo and threw that at him as well. He dodged that one also. "I'm going to keep throwing things until I find something to knock you out with. So keep standing in here if you want." She looked around the room for something else to throw.

"All right, all right. You don't want me to sleep in here tonight. That's fine; I'll go hang out with the kids. Just stop throwing things," he said as he walked out of the room and closed the door behind him.

Cassandra picked up the candy dish off the nightstand and threw it at the door. It crashed and shattered against the door just as the glass had. She sat down on her bed thinking about the fool she had been to let down her guard and trust JT Thomas with her heart again. She looked to heaven and said, "See where all this trusting has gotten me? I'm headed to court and will probably be in every newspaper in the city as the silly wife whose husband can't keep his pants up."

She had called this morning and cancelled her appointment for Tuesday with Dr. Clarkson. She'd thought that she and JT could work things out without the need of a therapist. But now it looked like she would have to call his secretary and reschedule her appointment. She needed to tell Dr. Clarkson that she had found her anger.

Fifteen

Margie and Diane were seated in comfortable black leather chairs in Luke Watson's office. Luke had agreed to represent them in their sexual abuse lawsuit against JT and Faith Outreach Church. Margie was fidgety, and her hands were shaking. Diane was popping gum and sitting in her chair like a mac.

"So what's next, Luke?" Diane asked.

Luke Watson looked at the paperwork on his desk before he spoke. "Well, I had the proper documents filed quickly like you asked. Someone at the church should have received them yesterday. I'm still waiting on a response from their attorney."

"How long is that going to take? I'm not trying to drag this out. I want everyone to know all about JT Thomas's womanizing *right now*," Diane said.

"These things take time, Mrs. Benson," Luke said.

"Why? When you file a lawsuit don't you get a court date?"

"Yes, we'll get a court date, but there's a lot we need to cover before we ever step in court. And I'll need the response back from Faith Outreach's attorney so that we'll know what their defense will be."

"JT has no defense. He's a mangy dog, and he likes sex. That's it, end of story," Diane said.

"That may very well be the case, but I guarantee you the

response will not say anything like that. And you need to remember we have alleged that Faith Outreach is just a culpable as JT because they allowed his behavior. They may have a very different take on that, and we need to see what they are going to say," Luke tried to explain.

"Whatever." Diane waved her hand in the air as if dismissing Luke's comment. "I don't see why we just can't contact every television station in Cleveland and tell them all about what JT did to us."

Margie had been quietly listening to the back and forth exchange between Diane and Mr. Watson. But when Diane mentioned contacting the television stations, she raised her hand as if she were in school and needed permission to speak.

Luke turned to Margie. "You have something you want to say?"

Margie cleared her throat and nervously said, "I-I didn't agree to go on television. I want this handled as quietly as possible."

Diane swiveled around in her seat. "Margie, now you need to stop being a doormat. You were misused by that man more than anyone else. You should be thrilled about having him exposed for the devil he is."

"I'm not out for vengeance. I only want justice. I agree that JT owes me, but that's no reason to drag the man and his family in the gutter."

"You're still in love with him." Diane spat the words at Margie.

"No. I realize that what JT and I had wasn't love." She also knew that what she had at home wasn't much closer to love either. Love was offered to everyone else but her; until she gave birth to Marissa. Thinking of Marissa gave her power. With conviction she told Diane, "I have a child, and I don't want her hearing about all of this and being ashamed of her mother."

"Who's the mama, you or her? I've got kids too, and if they ask me anything about my business, I just tell them to stay in a child's place and get out of my face," Diane told her with her hands on her hips. "You don't let kids run your life. That just doesn't make sense."

"Actually, Margie makes a very good point. I think both of you ladies need to talk with your children if they are old enough to understand what's going on, and you need to make sure your husbands are okay with how a case like this will affect their lives," Luke told them.

"I'm not married," Margie said with the same look of shame she'd carried since she allowed Tony to move in with her. But as she left her attorney's office, she decided that she did owe Tony the courtesy of knowing what a case against JT could mean for them. Yeah, Tony was fine with the lawsuit. He wanted to help her spend the money. But did he want it blasted across every news station in Cleveland that the mother of his child had an affair with a married preacher?

She had signed up with a temp agency and was supposed to go to their offices after the meeting in Luke's office, but she took a detour home so that she could talk to Tony first. She pulled up in front of their apartment and got out of the car. Tony had been laid off from his job over a year ago and hadn't been able to find employment since. But what bugged Margie was the fact that she still had to take Marissa to the daycare even though she knew Tony had given up looking for work six months ago. All he did now was sit in the house, finding friends on Myspace and Facebook.

"Tony," she yelled as she opened the front door. She picked up two glasses and two dirty plates off the coffee table in the living room and took them to the kitchen. He was such a slob. Margie didn't understand why he couldn't clean up after himself since he was home all day making the mess in the first place.

As she stood by the sink, she heard whispering in her bedroom, as if Tony was talking to someone, but didn't want her to hear. She walked out of the kitchen and tried to open her bedroom door. It was locked. "Tony, what's going on in there?" she asked.

The whispering stopped, but Tony didn't answer her.

She shook the knob. "Open the door. Who are you talking to in my bedroom?"

Still no response.

"Don't make me break this door down, Tony."

She heard someone on the other side of the door whisper, "What are we going to do?"

"You're going to open this door and get out of my apartment. That's what you're going to do," Margie shouted.

The door opened and Tony stood in front of her, no shirt on; pants unzipped. The woman behind Tony had a yellow button down dress on, but her feet were bare. She had this terrified look on her face as if she were playing a part in the movie Obsessed, and Margie was about to beat her down.

Margie was normally very reserved. She'd been raised in church by a God fearing mother who taught her to wear long dresses and not to cross her legs when seated on the front row. She'd stopped wearing long dresses when she became an unwed mother, and she'd not only crossed her legs on the front pew, she'd slept with the pastor.

Beyond that, Margie had given up her church, her dignity, and her relationship with her mother was now in tatters all for the love of this man standing in front of her with a shoeless woman behind him. So Margie was about ready to let loose and beat this girl until she never wanted to steal another woman's man. "You've got about five seconds to get out of my apartment," Margie told the woman.

"Where am I supposed to go?" Tony asked

"I wasn't talking to you. I was talking to that thang standing behind you," Margie said as she reached her arm into her room, trying to grab a handful of the woman's long red hair. Tony grabbed her arm as the woman ran past him, picked her shoes up out of the living room, and ran out of the front door.

Margie pulled her arm out of Tony's grasp and said, "It's going to take you more than five seconds to pack your stuff. But I need you to go also."

He picked his T-shirt up off the floor and put it on. "What about Marissa? I guess you think you can raise her on your own."

"That's what I've been doing," she said as she walked away from her bedroom. She couldn't inhale the smells that were coming out of that room one second longer, so she sat down in the living room and put her head in her hands. She had loved Tony and had given up everything to be with him. Within the past few months she had come to understand that he didn't care as deeply for her as she did for him. But she'd never imagined that he would disrespect her by having another woman in the place where she paid all the bills.

"Oh, I don't help. Is that what you're trying to say?" Tony spat.

"When's the last time you paid child support, Tony? And to think, I was nice enough to tell the child support enforcement agency that you lived with me and was helping provide for Marissa so they could stop the child support order."

He was in the living room standing in front of the couch now. "You weren't lying. I do live here."

She looked up at him and said, "Not anymore you don't. I'm tired, Tony. You won't get a job. I'm paying all the bills, and now I come home and find you sleeping with some woman in my bed!"

"So I don't help out around here?"

"Are you listening to anything I've said? I just caught you with another woman in my bed. Do you really think I care that you do the dishes and take out the trash?" She rolled her eyes and flung her hands in the air. "Just get out."

"So that's how it is, huh? You're getting ready to get all this money because you slept with a married preacher, and suddenly, you don't need me around anymore."

His words stung. Yes, she had indeed gone against all her mother's teachings and fallen into the arms of a married man. She had hurt Cassandra just as this mystery woman she'd just found in her bedroom had hurt her. Her mother always said, 'You reap what you sow, little girl. So make sure you sow seeds you want to reap on yourself one day.' Oh, she was reaping all right. But it wasn't from the money she was going to get from a lawsuit. Margie was reaping all the wrong she'd done and she didn't like it one bit.

Diane was ticked off by Luke's suggestion that she discuss this lawsuit with her husband. But as she left her attorney's office and thought about the fact that Joe was footing the bill for her attorney, she'd thought better of talking things over with him. She still wasn't going to let him tell her what to do though. What did she care what Joe had a problem with? He should just be glad she was back home and helping him take care of them brats.

She pulled into the parking lot and rolled her eyes as she noted that people still weren't buying cars. Joe had scrapped and saved in order to buy this car dealership five years ago. Money was flowing into their hands left and right in those days. But when the economy tanked, folks stopped buying cars and Joe had to get a second job. Since he could build a house from scratch, he'd gotten an evening job at Lowe's in the lumber department. But things were still tight, so Diane was thinking about suggesting that he get another job. Jamaicans worked a bunch of jobs, why couldn't he?

Joe was on the showroom floor talking to a guy that looked as if he couldn't count to ten, let alone come up with the ten grand needed to purchase that marked down Capri. She walked over to him and said, "We need to talk."

Joe had been explaining the features of the car to his customer when Diane approached. He turned to her and said, "Why don't you wait in my office, honey. I'll be there in a minute."

Diane put her hands on her hips; neck bobbed as her eyes bulged out of her head. She just knew this man had lost his mind. Keep her waiting so he could talk to this as-soon-as-my-luck-turns-I'll-buy-a-car-so-called-customer? "I don't have all day, Joe."

"Look, if this is a bad time, I could always just take your business card and get back in touch with you," the customer said.

"No sir, you came at the right time. I'm sure my wife will give us a few more minutes to discuss your interest in this car." He turned back to Diane and asked again, "Can you please wait for me in my office?"

Diane huffed as she turned around and walked out of the showroom. She didn't have time to wait on Joe. Her schedule was just as busy as his. He thought that she didn't have any-thing to do just because she worked at home. But housewives were just as busy as working husbands.

As she drove out of the lot, Diane picked up her cell phone and dialed Mattie. "Did my attorney contact you about next week?" she asked as soon as Mattie said hello.

"Who is this?" Mattie asked.

"Don't play games. You know who you're talking to."

"Well, don't call my house acting so informal. You and I are not best friends. So you need to identify yourself before asking me questions."

"Okay," Diane said, taking a deep breath and rolling her eyes. "Hello, Mattie, this is Diane. I was calling to find out if my attorney contacted you about the preliminary hearing next week?"

"Ain't that what you pay him to do?"

"Of course, Mattie, but I forgot to ask him if he'd been able to reach you. You know the Bible says that we should be good stewards. So I'm just trying to handle my business."

"Don't that Bible of yours also say treat people how you want to be treated?"

"Yeah, it sure does," Diane answered, happy that she knew about at least two scriptures.

"Well, I don't bother you, so don't bother me."

Diane rolled her eyes. Why did she have to deal with this old hateful woman? "Look, Mattie, can you just tell me if my attorney contacted you or not?"

"If that'll get you off my phone, then yeah, he called. And I remembered every lie you asked me to tell, so you don't have to keep calling here. I told you before; I don't like you, and the less I speak to you the better." Mattie hung the phone up in Diane's ear after saying those sweet words.

Shaking her head at the audacity of the mean old woman she was forced to deal with, Diane put her cell phone back in her purse. She didn't have time to worry about crazy Mattie, talking about she had asked her to lie. What lie? All she asked Mattie to say was that Cassandra mistreated Lily and JT ignored her. Diane couldn't imagine Cassandra not mistreating a child that had been forced on her due to her husband's infidelity. Mattie wanted to play games and act like her child was too much of an angel to mistreat a child. Ha... whatever. Mattie could believe what she wanted, just as long as she said what Diane had told her to say. She didn't care and wouldn't spend another second worrying about Mattie Daniels. Her judge show would be on at two o'clock, and if she rushed home, she would just make it in time to watch that fine Judge Mathis bringing down the gavel.

Sixteen

Cassandra sat across from JT at the dinner table glaring at him. JT had put the kids to bed and slept on the couch the night before because Cassandra refused to come out of the bedroom after their argument. He wished there was something he could do to restore the joy she'd had this weekend. But she was afraid again. He could see it plain as he knew his name, but he was powerless to do anything about it.

"I talked to Lamont today," JT said, trying to draw Cassandra out.

Stabbing a few string beans with her fork, Cassandra kept her face directed toward her plate as she asked, "Did you ask him if you could borrow that money?"

"No. I already told you I wouldn't do that."

"No, not to save your family from being drug through the mud, you won't, but for your own selfish desires, like buying a Bentley you would spend money that you owed a friend."

"No I wouldn't. Not anymore. Look, Cassandra, you asked me to not just be a man but to be God's man. You can't have it both ways. I can't take what doesn't belong to me to get me out of a fix I put my own self into in the first place." When she didn't respond, he inhaled deeply, and then changed the subject. "Lamont is doing great. He almost has full use of his left arm back. He thinks he might be able to move down here in about two weeks."

"That soon."

"Yeah, he's ready to get away from his old surroundings and start fresh in a new city."

She cut a piece of her meatloaf with her fork, and then told JT, "This might not be the place for him, because the past has sure caught up to us. Maybe the same thing will happen to him if he moves in with us."

JT put down his fork. Cassandra's attitude had made him lose his appetite. And for a man used to shoveling his food in his mouth like he was trying to make the world record for eating the fastest; that was an accomplishment on Cassandra's part. "Will you please look at me?"

"What for, JT? What am I going to see that I haven't already?"

JT stood up, he grabbed Cassandra's arm and walked her into the living room. His children were napping in the family room, but he didn't want to run the risk of waking them up if he and Cassandra started arguing in the kitchen. They stood in front of each other, between the couch and love seat; Cassandra's eyes were averted. She looked first at JT's chest, then at the walls.

"I am not the enemy, Cassandra. And I promise you that I'm going to do everything I can to keep this lawsuit from affecting our family."

She was non-responsive as she continued staring off. If she had been lying down, JT would have called 911 so the paramedics could help him bring his wife back to life. But he didn't need paramedics, he needed Jesus. JT put Cassandra's hand in his and asked, "Would you pray with me?"

That got her attention. But only a little. She said, "Whatever."

They sat on the couch together, still holding hands as JT

called on the Lord to help them through this situation. He began by thanking the Lord for his family and telling Him how grateful he was that he'd been blessed so by God. He then called each child's name out to God and prayed a special blessing for each of them, and then he prayed for Cassandra. "Lord, I know that things have not always been easy for Cassandra. She's had to deal with a lot of things that no one should have to deal with; like discovering that her mom and dad had lied to her for so many years. Cassandra has lost a child, and then she had to deal with a cheating and neglectful husband. I will never be able to mend her heart from all that has happened, but Father, I do believe that you are the mender of broken hearts. So, I ask you to walk with Cassandra through this difficult time. Open her eyes so that she can see me clearly and know that with as much as is in my power, I will never break her heart again. Thank you, Jesus."

"Amen," Cassandra said, and then pulled her hands out of JT's.

He opened his eyes and looked at his wife. She appeared to have softened some. She had built that wall back up overnight, but he and the Lord would knock it down. "I wasn't finished praying, honey. If you don't mind, I wanted to pray for Diane and Margie also."

Cassandra stood and backed away from him. "No. Pray for them yourself. I don't want to hear it."

He reached for her, pulling her into his arms. "I'm sorry, honey. I didn't want to upset you." They stood there holding each other. Although JT did not say the words out loud, he did silently pray that God would give him the strength to ask Margie for forgiveness and that he would soon be able to forgive Diane for the things she had done to him.

But forgiveness for Diane would prove to be harder than

JT expected. The doorbell rang as he and Cassandra moved apart. When he opened the door, a white man he didn't recognize stood in front of him, looking like a bill collector.

"Jerome Tyler Thomas?" the man asked.

"That's me. Can I help you?" Jerome replied.

The man lifted the envelope he'd had in his hand. He handed it to JT and said, "You've been served."

"I've been served what?" JT asked as the man scurried off his porch.

Cassandra came up from behind him and closed the front door as JT opened the envelope. "What's that?"

He pulled the documents out of the envelope, quickly scanned them, and then told Cassandra, "Documents concerning Diane and Margie's case against me."

"Didn't they already send these documents to the church? Why do they have to come around our house?"

"Don't you get it, Cassandra? Diane wants to punish me. And she's going to use every weapon in her arsenal to make sure we don't get custody of Lily."

"She already slept with you. Why does she need to humiliate me by telling the world about all your dirty deeds? And why does she want to take Lily from us? She didn't even want that baby." Tears formed in her eyes, and her voice elevated as she said, "What's next, JT? Will Children Services walk up in here and take the rest of our kids too?"

"No, baby. Diane isn't going to take Lily, and no one else is going to take Jerome or Aaron either."

"I don't believe you." She looked at JT as if examining him. She plopped down on the couch and said, "Maybe Diane isn't punishing you at all. Maybe God hasn't forgiven you for all your wrongdoing, and this is just His way of standing back and allowing you to get everything that's coming to you. And if I continue to stay with you, then I'll keep going through right along with you."

JT stood behind the couch. He wanted to bend down and envelope Cassandra in his arms, but he figured she would just reject him. So he simply told her, "You're wrong, Sanni. God has forgiven me for everything. I can feel it in my soul. When I pray, God is listening. But it's not God's fault that I fooled around with Diane, so I can't blame Him for the things she's doing to us right now."

Tears streamed down Cassandra's face. "I'm tired, JT. I can't take anymore. I thought I could come back home, but maybe I was wrong. Maybe I don't belong here anymore."

JT walked around the couch and sat down next to his wife. Her head was bent and her shoulders slumped as she sobbed. He lifted her head, causing her to look at him as he said, "You belong right her. You've always belonged with me."

She pushed his hand away from her face.

"Trust me, Sanni. We'll make it through this."

"Shut up, JT. Just get out of my face," she said as she shoved him.

"What do you want me to do, Sanni? Tell me, and I'll do it."

She wiped the tears from her face, stood up, and walked away without responding to him.

JT jumped up and followed her. He grabbed her arm and tried to turn her back toward him. "Don't do this, Sanni. Be reasonable, and stop running away from me."

Cassandra swung around and hit her husband in the face with her fist. "If you wanted a reasonable wife, you should have been a faithful husband."

"I am faithful," JT protested as he held his jaw.

Cassandra's hands went to her hips. She had a smirk on

her face when she said, "You're a day late and a dollar short on that trick."

"I'm sorry, Sanni. But we will get through this; just have faith in me."

She rolled her eyes and lifted her hands in exasperation as she said, "Just go pray, JT. Pray that God gives me the strength to forgive you, Margie, and Diane before I go buy a gun."

Seventeen

Cassandra needed her mommy. But she had thrown Mommy out of her house because of the way she talked about JT. Today, she would give anything to sit on the couch with her mom and listen as she ripped into her husband. But she knew her mother all too well. Mattie would go way too far, saying things against JT that Cassandra knew weren't true, and then she would end up defending him. She didn't want to defend JT, so she was going to stay away from her mother for at least another week. Then she would call and let the boys talk to her.

Right now, she was sitting in Dr. Clarkson's office, waiting on him to tell her that she was being ridiculous and that she should go home and help her husband through this difficult time. But he didn't do that. Dr. Clarkson got up from his comfortable listening chair, which was positioned next to the couch his clients sat or laid on. He sat down behind his desk, opened his desk drawer and pulled out a business card. He walked back over to Cassandra and said, "I think you should contact Dr. Sandra Neumann."

Cassandra looked at the card Dr. Clarkson handed her with confusion in her eyes. "I was just telling you that I'm thinking about leaving my husband. What does this woman have to do with my decision?"

"I want to be honest with you, Cassandra. You came to me for help, but I have come to care for you a great deal."

"Whoa, wait a minute. Hold on," Cassandra said as she held up her hands, trying to halt this conversation.

"It's the truth, Cassandra. I realized when I met you for lunch and held your hand that I wasn't handling our relationship professionally. Even now, I want to encourage you to divorce your husband, because I'm hoping that I might have a chance with you. And that's not professional, and it's not right."

"I don't understand." Cassandra was totally caught off guard with this one. Yeah, JT had told her that Dr. Clarkson had a thing for her, but she hadn't believed that. She was a mom after all. She wasn't some diva who turned heads as she walked down the street. But now that she thought about it, she'd been surprised when JT, who looked more like a male model than a pastor, had been attracted to her.

Dr. Clarkson pointed at the card in Cassandra's hand. "Dr. Neumann is a much better therapist than I am, and she won't have ulterior motives."

Cassandra stood up. Anger was overtaking her again. She was conflicted. She had come in Dr. Clarkson's office wanting to bash JT's head in, but now she wished she had that iron skillet she fried chicken in, so she could knock Dr. Clarkson upside the head with it. "I'm your patient. I came to you for help. You shouldn't have ulterior motives either."

He lowered his head and told her, "I know. This has never happened to me before. I have always maintained a professional relationship with all of my clients." He raised his head and looked into her eyes as he continued, "The bottom line is this . . . I want to be with you. So I'm leaving the ball in your court. If you decide to divorce your husband, and if you'd like a friend; I'm here."

Cassandra stared at this man seated before her. This was

the first time she'd bothered to notice him as a man and not just her doctor. He was handsome—that is, if you considered Boris Kodjoe handsome; and Cassandra did. She allowed her mind to drift as she wondered about life after JT. Could she have a happy life with Dr. Clarkson even though she'd failed in her marriage to JT? Or would she just end up right back here, preparing for another divorce?

"Look, Dr. Clarkson, I'm flattered by the fact that you are attracted to me. But I'm not interested in ending one relationship just so I can begin another."

She walked out of his office and got in her car. As she sat behind the wheel, she slowly exhaled and looked to heaven. If she were honest with herself, she had been tempted by Dr. Clarkson's proposal, but God had made a way of escape for her. "Thank you, Jesus."

She drove home feeling as if she had more insight into how JT had sunk into adultery. Things were going bad at home, and so when the opportunity presented itself, he went for it, assuming that the grass would be greener. Cassandra had only imagined that her life might be better with Dr. Clarkson for a moment. She now could see how someone could be tricked by the devil. But she needed to hear it from JT's own lips. She now wanted to know how each affair began.

She knew this knowledge would hurt, and didn't know for sure whether it would be the thing to help her move forward in her marriage or the thing that would dot all the I's and crossed all the T's in her divorce decree.

"Are you sure you want to know this?" JT asked Cassandra when they were alone later that night.

"I don't *want* to know, JT. I need to know. See, when Dr.

Clarkson propositioned me this afternoon, I was tempted, but by the time I reached my car, I knew for a fact that God had helped me resist that temptation. So I need to know why God hadn't been able to help you, and whether I can trust that you will allow Him to help you in the future."

"Okay, well have a seat, because I can guarantee you're not going to like my answers, but I promise to be truthful."

Cassandra sat down on the couch in the family room and waited for JT to begin his saga.

"The first time I cheated on you was after our first child, Sarah, died. I was in so much pain and so angry with God that I didn't take time to think about what my actions would do to you. I just wanted the pain to go away. So when I started working with Margie on one of our church programs, I noticed how lonely she seemed."

"So you took advantage of her just like Dr. Clarkson tried to take advantage of the turmoil I'm going through? Maybe I should cut a page out of Margie and Diane's playbook and sue Dr. Clarkson."

"I don't think you can, babe. As much as I hate to admit it, he was honest about his feelings and even recommended that you see another therapist. That's more than I did for Margie. I lured her into an affair by playing on her emotions." He saw Cassandra wince at his words and wished that he could take not only his words back, but also his actions. "I'm sorry, honey, but it's true. If I'm going to face facts, the truth is, I wronged Margie more than either of the other women I slept with."

"Okay," Cassandra said slowly. "What about Diane? How did your affair with her begin?"

JT sat down across from Cassandra. He didn't want to sit on the couch next to her in case she decided to haul off and punch him like she did last night. "You see how she dresses in those short skirts and tight shirts that leave her breasts exposed for all of the world to see, right?"

"Yeah, I noticed that she looks like a hooker. But are you saying that I need to be worried about every scantly clothed woman that comes into the church?"

JT waved that suggestion off. "I'm not dressing it up, defending it, or trying to make it look like something it's not. I have more self-control than that. But Diane would come into my office bending over so I could see everything the Lord blessed her with. Then she started whispering in my ear. I told her time and time again that I wasn't interested."

Cassandra twisted her lips as if she didn't believe a word JT was saying. "Why weren't you interested?"

"I was trying to keep my word to you. After you found out about Margie, I promised you I wouldn't cheat again. And I really tried. But my relationship with God still wasn't repaired, so after months of telling Diane I wasn't interested, I finally gave in. It's been downhill for me ever since. The affair with Vivian even started as a result of Diane."

"And how was that?" Cassandra asked snippily.

"I told you that you weren't going to want to know all of this."

"Just keep going."

"All right, but I'm begging you to keep in mind that you asked me to tell you this stuff."

Cassandra rolled her eyes, but said nothing else.

"All right, the simplest way to say this is, Diane told Vivian about our affair so Vivian approached me. She wanted to know if I was through with Diane and if I wanted to start something with her. I was way off God's path by then and didn't know if I even wanted to find my way back, so I just let it happen. And now Bishop wants me to say that Margie came on to me just like Diane and Vivian did."

Cassandra scoffed. "He's probably still angry because you admitted that Lily was your child. We all know how he handles situations like that."

JT put his hand over his wife's in an attempt to comfort her. "He loves you, Sanni. Why won't you give the man a chance to prove it?"

Rolling her eyes, she removed her hands from JT's hold. She sat in silence for a moment, then turned back to JT with another question. "Can I ask you something, JT?"

"Are you going to throw anything at me?"

Cassandra laughed. "Not tonight. I think I broke up enough of my stuff the other night."

"Laughter looks good on you, Sanni. I wish I had been able to put a thousand more smiles on your face."

In spite of herself, she blushed. "Don't try to charm me, JT."

"Okay. What's your question?"

"Do you think that since Diane and Vivian came onto you, that you are a victim? Or can you tell me who the real victims are?"

"If Diane hadn't pursued me the way she did, I never would have cheated with her. So in a way, I want to say that I'm the victim. But I can't let go of the fact that I was her pastor and therefore should have raised up the standard that she needed to follow." He shook his head, and then looked to Cassandra with questioning eyes. "I don't know, Sanni. Can we both be victims of the same crime, or does there have to be one victim per crime?"

"Wrong answer," she said as she stood up and walked out of the room.

Eighteen

Margie was distraught. Things were spiraling out of control and she didn't know how to stop them. She wanted to talk to her mother and just sit and listen as she imparted wisdom like she did when she was a little girl. But her mother had told her not to call until she had come back to her right mind. The thing was, she couldn't call her mother anyway. Margie's phone had been turned off. And when she and Marissa arrived home today, she discovered that an eviction notice had been taped to her front door. She pulled it off the door and went inside.

Tony was lying on the couch resting from his busy day of being a TV critic. He had refused to leave her apartment, claiming that he needed a few days to find a place. She laid the eviction notice on the dining room table and went into her bedroom.

Tony followed her into the bedroom and took Marissa out of her arms. "Hey, little one; how was your day?"

Marissa smiled brightly. "Daddy!"

"That's right baby, Daddy's home."

Where else would he be? Margie thought as she rolled her eyes heavenward. It wasn't like he was out working, or heaven forbid, looking for work. And if she heard him say one more time how there just weren't any jobs out there when she saw help wanted signs everyday as she drove passed McDonalds and Burger King, she would lose her mind.

"Hey, did you see that eviction notice?" Tony asked her while bouncing Marissa on his hip.

"Sure did," Margie said as she opened the closet door and took out her suitcase.

"Do you think we could ask your mom for some help? She might be a stubborn old lady, but I doubt that she would want to see her grandchild on the street."

"That's what I'm hoping," Margie answered as she opened her top drawer, took her under garments out, and then threw them in her suitcase. She then started pulling clothes out of her closet and stuffed as much as would fit.

"Why are you packing? We just got the eviction notice. They have to take us to court before we have to leave this place."

He would know. When she met him, he had just been evicted. He'd confided that he'd been evicted from three previous places. Her heart had gone out to him then, thinking that no matter how hard he tried, he just couldn't get a break. Now she knew that a person had to go out and make their own breaks. Breaks don't just knock on the front door while you're sitting in the living room watching TV.

She went into Marissa's room and took her suitcase out. She repeated the same process of throwing under garments and whatever clothes would fit in her suitcase.

"What are you doing?" he asked again.

She looked at him as she pulled Marissa's suitcase off the bed, but didn't respond. She then grabbed her suitcase and took them both to her car. She came back in, picked up her purse and held out her hand for Tony to give Marissa to her.

"Answer me," he said as he refused to give Marissa to her.

"Give me my baby, Tony."

"Give me an answer. I have a right to know where you're taking my daughter."

She put her hands on her hips. She thought about refusing to answer, but she didn't want to prolong this thing with Tony any longer than she needed to. "I'm going to do as you suggested; ask my mother for help."

"Then why'd you pack suitcases?"

She snatched Marissa out of his arms as she said, "Because I need her to help me and Marissa, not you."

"Oh, so it like that, huh? You gon' leave me when the chips are down after all I've done for you?"

"More like all you've done to me," she said as she turned and walked out the door.

He followed her to the car, screaming and yelling at her for all the neighbors to hear. She didn't care. Margie was determined that if she got away from Tony today, she would never come back to him. This was it for her. She was chocking this up as a life lesson and moving on.

Marissa was crying as Margie strapped her into her car seat. She closed the back door and turned back to Tony. "Can you please stop yelling at the top of your lungs? You're scaring Marissa."

To his credit, Tony looked in the backseat, saw the tears running down Marissa's face, and then lowered his voice. However, what he said was just as mean as when he had been yelling. "Go on, then. I don't need you. I got plenty of women, and they all look better than you ever could."

She walked around the car, trying to get away from his insults. Tony grabbed a handful of her hair and yanked. "Stop, Tony; that hurts," she said as she tried to get his hand out of her hair, but he kept yanking it. "Stop, I just want to leave."

"You'll leave when I tell you to leave," he said with his mouth pressed against her ear. "I only hooked up with you because you looked lonely and pathetic. I knew you would take care of me and you did."

"Is he bothering you?" Her next door neighbor came out on the porch with cell phone in hand. "Do I need to call the police?"

Tony let her go then. "You need to mind your own business," he told the woman.

Margie took that opportunity to jump in her car and lock the doors. She waved and mouthed thank you to the woman as she started her car and drove off. Marissa was still crying. She reached back and touched her daughter's leg as she drove. "There, there, sweet baby; we're okay."

But then as she thought about how life had turned so wrong on her, she changed her statement to, "I hope we're going to be okay."

Life had been so much simpler when she was in church; before she started sleeping with JT. If she had to pinpoint when things started going wrong for her, it would have been that first night JT talked her into having sex with him. Things looked fine at first. Margie thought she had gotten rid of that lonely feeling that she seemed to be carrying around. But when JT had to get up and go home to his wife, she was lonely all over again. Sleeping with JT hadn't fixed anything for her, it just made it worse. She came to a red light, stopped the car and hit the steering wheel with her fist as she thought about the fact that JT never even apologized to her for making her believe that they could ever have a life together when all the time he knew that he would never leave his wife.

But how had she fallen for all his tricks in the first place? If she had been as sold out to the Lord as she thought she had been, would JT have been able to seduce her? She pulled up in the driveway of her mother's home. She pushed all thoughts of her own culpability out of her mind as she thought about the fact that the affair with JT had been the beginning of her strained relationship with her mother.

Betty Milner was the sweetest woman on earth. She'd taught Margie how to cook and how to love the Lord her God. Her mother had taken her on trips around the world because she wanted Margie to experience life outside of Cleveland. And when the time came, Betty Milner gave up vacationing in order to pay Margie's college tuition.

Tears sprang to Margie's eyes as she thought of the day her mother told her that she wouldn't step foot in her house again until she got right with the Lord.

"Why can't you accept me the way I am?" Margie had asked.

"I will never accept the fact that a child of mine is dead set on spending eternity in hell." Betty picked up her purse and said, *"Call me when you get right with God and throw that bum out of your house."*

Well, she hadn't gotten right with God. But she had gotten rid of Tony. Maybe one out of two would be good enough for her mother. She hoped so, anyway. She took Marissa out of her car seat, grabbed their suitcases, and then knocked on her mother's front door.

"I'm coming," Betty yelled from somewhere within the house.

Hearing her mother's voice brought more tears to her eyes. And as the door opened, the tears were flowing down her face. Her mother only opened the door a crack. Margie feared that she might close it in her face and she couldn't deal with that right now. She opened her mouth and blubbered. "I-I don't have anywhere else to go. We need your help."

The door opened wider, and Betty held out her arms to embrace her daughter and granddaughter.

Nineteen

JT sat in his office at the community center going over his agenda for the following week when someone knocked on his door. He put the papers aside and said, "Come in."

The door opened, and Ellen Peoples walked in wearing a leopard print dress that clung to her curves and wouldn't let go. JT sat up in his chair and braced himself. He hoped he had misjudged her the other Sunday, but he couldn't help but be suspicious about this visit. "Mrs. Peoples, right?"

"Why don't you call me, Ellen," she said as she walked closer to his desk and stood in front of him.

"I probably should stick with Mrs. Peoples for now."

"Suit yourself," she said as she sat down and crossed her long legs. The slit in the dress widened so that JT had a full view of her legs and much more if he chose to look.

"What can I do for you?" he asked, being mindful to look her in the eyes and nowhere else.

"I stopped by because I think I left my Bible after service the other day."

"The janitor normally leaves a log of items that were left in the auditorium on my desk." He shuffled some papers around until he found what he was looking for, and then scanned it. "No Bibles this week. We normally get a lot of those on the list, but not this week," he said as he looked back up at her.

"Oh, well maybe I left it in my husband's car or something." She scooted forward in her seat, leaned closer to JT and said, "I really stopped in to see you anyway. I enjoyed your sermon, and I've heard a lot about you."

Same game, just a different day as far as JT was concerned. He'd been through this before, and he wasn't about to let this go any further. He straightened in his seat as he told her, "I'm not sure what you heard, but if you thought I was interested in you, you're wrong."

She licked her lips and lifted her chest. "Well, now that you mention it, I did feel something electric when we shook hands. I know you felt it also. I saw the look on your face."

JT stood up. "If you saw a strained expression on my face, it was because I thought you held my hand too long, and I think I know you from somewhere. I just can't place where we've met before."

Ellen shook her head. "No way, baby. If we'd met before, as fine as you are, I would have remembered it."

JT walked over to his office door and opened it. ""I'm Pastor Thomas to you. Only my wife calls me baby." He wished his wife would call him baby. She was too busy throwing things at his head, but even so, he wanted nothing to do with the woman in front of him. He didn't care how fine she was, he was satisfied with what he had at home. Even while they were suffering through bad times. "I need you to leave my office," JT told her.

Ellen swiveled around in her seat. "What? Why on earth would I leave? I just got here."

"I have work to do, and I'm not interested in what you're offering. I'm a married man, and I will not disrespect my wife by entertaining you one second longer."

"I'm a married woman. What's the big deal?"

"You wouldn't even understand if I told you," JT said as he swept his hand in the direction of the door. "Now get out."

Ellen huffily got out of her seat and strutted toward the door. She stopped when she was standing next to him and said, "I'll give you time. You're worth the wait."

"You'll be waiting in vain, Mrs. Peoples. So I suggest that you and your husband find another church to attend if I'm your motive for attending mine." He closed the door as she slithered out of it.

As he sat back down behind his desk, JT felt like a piece of meat hanging in a slaughter house; waiting for meat eaters to come bid on him. But then he remembered Cassandra's question. *Who is the victim?* He also remembered how she told him he'd given the wrong answer when he speculated over whether he or Diane had been the victim in their affair. Now he understood what she had meant. He'd just told Ellen that he wouldn't disrespect his wife by entertaining her. And that's when he had gotten a glimpse of the real victims of affairs. It wasn't the two grown folks who willingly walked into it with both eyes open. Diane wasn't a victim and neither was he. Joe and his children had become the victims of Diane's affairs just as Cassandra and his children had. The knowledge of that broke JT's heart. It was him; he had single handedly tore his family apart. When his son got older and had to explain to school friends how they had a sister, but their mother wasn't her mother; they would be wounded. They might not let others see their wounds, but they would show up sooner or later. And it would be his fault.

From this day forward, JT determined that he would do everything within his power to right the wrongs of his past. He would build a strong bond with his wife and children and pray that his misdeeds didn't stop them from becoming everything they were meant to be. In short, he was determined to make his family proud. And he would start by telling the truth.

He turned off the lights in his office and headed over to Faith Outreach Church. He had to give a deposition for the lawsuit today. Tom Albright, the attorney for Faith Outreach, wouldn't like what JT had to say. But JT wasn't thinking about him. Making his family proud might hurt in the short term, but if they got through this, they would all be better for his willingness to stand on the truth.

Tom Albright looked at JT with astonishment in his eyes for a moment. He turned off the recorder, and then said, "Now look, Pastor Thomas, this is a delicate issue. You can't just say that you took advantage of Margie Milner and not expect her to walk away with even more money than she's already asked for."

"It's the truth. What else can I say?"

The session was being taped, but Tom looked through his notes before telling JT, "We can handle this situation with you and Diane Benson. I like the information you've given us on her. She is going to be seen as a liar the moment she opens her mouth, but we simply cannot have you admit to luring Margie Milner into an affair. Think about Faith Outreach, Pastor. This money will be coming out of the church's pockets, not yours."

"Why does the money have to come from Faith Outreach? I was suspended from my duties when Bishop found out what I was doing." JT waved a hand in the air as if dismissing the whole thing. "Look, why don't I just get my own attorney? That way, you, as Faith Outreach's attorney, can admit to knowing that what I did was wrong, but tell the judge that the church had nothing to do with the things I did."

"That's the way I wanted to handle this situation," Tom admitted.

"Then that's what I'll do," JT said as he rose out of his seat.

"Wait a minute. Please sit back down, Pastor Thomas."

JT's left brow arched, but he sat back down.

"Bishop Turner has requested that we do everything within our power to help you through this. Now, although I may think that the best thing for Faith Outreach would be to wash their hands of you, they have chosen to stand by you."

"I don't need them to do this for me. Especially if you want me to lie about the way things happened. I'm through with all that lying and scheming." He was God's man, and JT was determined to act like it. He didn't know where he would get a million dollars to pay Diane and Margie, but he wouldn't take a dime from the money he owed Lamont. And if the church ended up paying his debt, JT would work three or four jobs to pay them back every cent. But he would not lie to get himself out of this jam.

"I guess we're done for the day then. I need to speak with Bishop Turner to see how he wants to proceed, and then I'll let you know what we're going to do."

"Fair enough, man." JT stood up and shook hands with Tom. "Thanks for taking care of this for the church."

"You know I love this place. I'm going to get us out of this," Tom said with a smile.

JT walked out of the office and found Unders in the sanctuary. He was seated in the front row, staring up at the pulpit. JT sat down next to him and tried to figure out what he was looking at. When he saw nothing out of the ordinary he asked, "What's up there?"

Pastor Unders looked at JT for a moment, and then turned his face back to the pulpit. "I was just thinking about the things expected of a preacher and how weighty the burden is sometimes."

Unders words caused JT to turn back to the pulpit area. He had preached in this room for five years, but he had never been more aware of the cost of the position as he was right now, sitting in the pews staring at the wooden pulpit with Unders beside him. "Weighty indeed," JT agreed.

They sat there in silence for a moment, and then JT said, "I told the truth during my deposition. I let Tom know that I wouldn't lie, no matter what Bishop wanted me to do. And I'm sorry, Unders, but what I did just may cost the church a lot of money. But I promise you, I'll pay it back."

Unders smiled for the first time since JT sat down with him. "I don't care about the money, JT. I'm just glad that you told the truth. I told Bishop I wasn't going to lie about this situation either. He's not happy, but that's that."

"I don't want you to lie for me, Unders. I'm a grown man. I can handle myself."

"I've been worried about you ever since this thing began. I've been praying for you and Cassandra."

Before JT could respond, Max Moore walked into the sanctuary and loudly interrupted them. JT stood and clasped hands with him. "Man, what are you doing here?"

"Unders asked me to meet with the attorney today to tell them what a wonderful man you are," Max said with a smirk. "I should tell him how you used to steal my church members."

"You better not."

"I'm just joking, man. I got nothing but love for you."

"Thanks, I need my brothers in Christ with me right now. At least that means I've got somebody on my side."

Max looked at him quizzically. "Problems with Cassandra?"
JT nodded.

"I thought things had gotten better for you and Cassandra."

"Yeah, me too. But the other night she told me I needed to pray that she didn't go buy a gun," JT said.

"See, I knew there was a reason I was praying," Unders said.

Max wasn't thinking about praying. He leaned his head back and roared. He laughed so hard tears rolled down his cheek.

JT rolled his eyes. "Thanks for the support."

"I'm sorry, man." Max straightened himself up as best he could. "But I got an image in my head of sweet Cassandra chasing you down the street like it was hunting season or something. Too funny."

As far as JT knew, Max had always been faithful to his wife, so he'd never experienced the awful pain of looking into the eyes of the woman he loved and seeing disappointment and mistrust. He hoped that Max would always be able to laugh about things like this, and that he would never know pain so deep that funny just wasn't funny anymore.

Twenty

Diane picked up the phone and dialed JT's house. She waited until Cassandra answered the phone, and then the heavy breathing started.

"Who is this?" she heard Cassandra ask.

Diane didn't answer, she just kept breathing until Cassandra slammed the phone in her ear. Diane hit the END button on her house phone, then leaned back against her comfy pillow in her king size bed and laughed her head off. Since she'd been back home, Diane had made it her business to call Cassandra twice a week. She wasn't checking in on Lily or asking for visitation. No, Diane just called and breathed into the phone. She figured that would good and irritate the *Queen of Thomas Manor*. Since they had a block on their house phone and all their calls appeared as private in the caller ID, she could harass Cassandra as much as she wanted.

Cassandra thought she was so perfect. Well, Diane couldn't wait until they went to court for their custody hearing and Ms. Perfect had to sit there and listen to her own mother tell the judge how unfit she really was. She rolled her eyes as she sat up on the side of the bed. Enough about Cassandra; Diana needed to get up and do some work around the house before she left for her appointment.

She scrolled down the contact list in her cell phone and pressed the button that connected her with the love of her life. When Brian Johnson answered the phone she said, "Are you still mad at me?"

"What do you think?" he said, and then hung up the phone.

She dialed him right back, and this time when he answered, she hurriedly said, "Baby, please don't hang up. I really need to talk to you."

"So talk," Brian said.

His anger crossed the line loud and clear to her, but she had to make him listen. "I've been trying to talk to you all week, but you keep hanging up. I know that you moved back here last week, but you didn't even call me."

"What was I suppose to do, Diane? Ask your husband to pass you the phone so I could tell you what's new in my life?"

"It's not even like that with me and Joe. We're more like roommates," she told him as she bent down and picked up the boxers Joe had discarded before climbing into bed last night. "He sleeps downstairs and I sleep upstairs. We're just trying to do the right thing for our children."

Brian harrumphed.

"What's that noise all about," Diane asked.

"You know what it's about. You tell Joe I said, he might want to get a DNA test to find out if the kids you stuck him with really are his," Brian said, just before hanging up in her face again.

Diane didn't understand Brian at all. He was the one who had convinced her that Lily was JT's kid in the first place. But she wasn't going to stand around worrying about Brian Johnson all day long. She would have him back in her arms soon enough. Right now she had to clean the house, and then go to her custody hearing. She couldn't wait to see the expression on JT and Cassandra's face when they realized what was about to happen to them. She was actually giddy with anticipation.

***

As Cassandra slammed down the phone in the face of her prank caller she realized something pretty wonderful and it made her smile. A couple weeks ago when she'd answered her phone and a breather was on the line, she'd had a panic attack. With all the money she'd wasted on her lousy therapist, who'd tried to convince her that she was having panic attacks because she was angry... she'd discovered that her panic attacks were because of fear. She'd prayed that weekend for God to release the fear from her heart, and even with all the drama she'd endured since that weekend, she hadn't had a single panic attack.

She wanted to call JT and tell him that she had made progress. That even though some woman, most likely Diane, was calling their house doing all this heavy breathing, she didn't immediately jump to thoughts of adultery. But she couldn't call JT, because even though she wasn't having panic attacks anymore, she was now having mad-black-woman attacks. She wanted to throw something at his head each time he walked through the door.

She had come back to her husband because she believed in her heart that he had changed. And she still believed that today. The problem was that the circumstances around him hadn't changed. He'd still hurt and misused people in the past, and it seemed like they were all trying to get back at him now. Meanwhile, JT was busy trying to make things right with the people he had hurt, but was somehow making things all wrong at home in the process. Cassandra still didn't understand why he couldn't borrow the money he owed Lamont and get them out of this jam. But no, all of a sudden JT was Mr. Do-The-Right-Thing. As far as Cassandra was concerned, JT picked the wrong time to have a conscious. She wanted her family spared the humiliation of going to court over her husband manipulating women into having sex with them.

As she sat down on the edge of her bed, the smile was gone from her face. Fresh tears now filled her eyes and threatened to spill over. There were days when Cassandra wanted to pack her bags and leave. Then, other days, she wanted to forget about everything that was going on and just enjoy her husband. Then JT walked through the door, she saw his face, and instead of running into his arms, her mind put a choke hold on her heart as it remembered the anger she felt at having to go to court over custody for a child she loved, but wished didn't belong to Diane Benson. This other court case concerning JT's womanizing wasn't making her feel any better toward him either.

For the second time that week, Cassandra wanted her mommy. She and Mattie hadn't talked in three weeks, and she truly missed her mother's companionship. Cassandra hoped that her mother had cooled down enough to talk to her, because she really needed a friend right now.

She picked up the phone and dialed Mattie. It rang five times, and then her answering machine picked up. Cassandra almost hung up, but then she decided to leave a message. "Hey, Mom, I was just calling to check on you. I hope you're not over there eating a bunch of fried foods. You know you're not supposed to have all that grease with your high blood pressure." The line beeped letting her know she had used up all her message space, so she hung up, grabbed her purse and key, then put the kids in the car. She was headed to Lily's custody hearing. JT was going to meet her there, so she dropped the kids off at Ms. Shirley's and headed to the courthouse.

Cassandra would be so happy when this was all over. Just when things had started to turn around for her and JT, she was back to having this love/hate relationship. In her heart Cassandra knew that Diane had orchestrated this other case against JT just so she could win the custody battle. And now she and her children would suffer so Diane could settle a score that she should never have had to settle in the first place. If JT hadn't been sleeping around, none of this would be happening to her. That's why Cassandra was barely speaking to her husband now. She blamed him for this nightmare she was enduring, and she wouldn't be able to think about repairing her relationship until the judge ruled in their favor.

"Please, Lord, let him rule in our favor." Lily had become a part of her. If they lost her, Cassandra knew it would be like when they lost their first daughter. She didn't know if she and JT would be able to bounce back from another blow like that. They had barely recovered from the loss of Sarah.

When she arrived at the courthouse, Cassandra parked her car and walked into the building. Cassandra thought fear would grip her and that she would have a panic attack the moment she opened the door. But she was surprisingly calm as she walked to Courtroom B. She smiled as she remembered all that praying she had done last night. She might be afraid of the outcome of their custody battle, but God had eased her fears; He had been doing that a lot for her lately. Even through this whole ordeal of JT being accused of manipulating women into having sex with him and listening to her husband admit that he had manipulated Margie, Cassandra might have been angry, but she hadn't lost control of her emotions enough to go into one of those awful panic attacks.

Rounding the corner, Cassandra saw her mother seated in a chair outside of Courtroom B. She rushed over to her and said, "Hey, did you get my message?"

Mattie didn't look up. She pretended to be searching for

something in her purse. "I didn't get no message from you, Cassandra Ann. The last time I talked to you, I was told not to come near your house again."

Cassandra sat down next to Mattie and put her arm around her shoulder. "I know, Mom. But I've missed you. I wanted to talk to you so bad these last few weeks. But I didn't know how you would respond to me. Can we please work something out?"

Mattie did look at Cassandra now. Her gaze was hard as she said, "You miss me, huh? Is that man of yours cattin' around again?"

Cassandra stood up. "Mother, that's uncalled for. Can you please try to be reasonable? I miss you, Mother." Cassandra put her hand on her chest as she continued, "Me, your daughter. I want a relationship with you."

Before Mattie could respond, JT came around the corner with their attorney, Tom Albright. "Get away from her, Cassandra," JT said.

Cassandra looked to her husband, and then back at her mother with an apologetic look on her face. She didn't care what problems they had with her mother, she could not tolerate JT thinking that he could turn her against her own mother. She was about to let him have it when he said, "Tom got the updated witness list this morning. Your mother is testifying for Diane."

"That's not true," was all Cassandra could say. Then she turned back to her mother with a questioning look. "What are you doing here? I didn't tell you I was coming here when I left the message on your answering machine."

The door to Courtroom B opened, and they were ushered into the room. JT grabbed hold of Cassandra's arm and moved her away from Mattie so they could take their seats in the plaintiff chairs. "What's going on, JT?" she asked when they were seated.

"I have no idea. Mattie's name had been added to the witness list about two weeks ago, but Tom didn't get an updated version until this morning."

Diane and Joe walked in with their attorney and sat down in the defendants' seats. Cassandra saw Diane swivel around in her seat and smile at Mattie. Cassandra stood up. JT tried grabbing her arm to get her to sit back down since the judge was now being seated. But Cassandra brushed him off. As the bailiff was asking everyone to rise, Cassandra walked over to her mother and said, "I want to know what's going on?"

Mattie didn't respond. The bailiff was trying to provide instructions about their case when Cassandra yelled, "Why are you doing this? What earthly reason could you have for being Diane's witness?"

The bailiff walked over to Cassandra and said, "Ma'am, if you don't sit down, you will have to leave the room."

Cassandra looked at the bailiff. She wanted to tell him that in normal circumstances she would never disrupt any type of proceeding. But her mother was here, and she was a witness for the defense. Instead of going into her sorrows, Cassandra turned away from them and sat back down next to JT.

He grabbed her hand and held onto it tightly. "Don't worry, Sanni. God is on our side."

She closed her eyes and massaged her temples with her free hand. She hoped and prayed that JT was right. She was sick and tired of people betraying her and getting away with it. She silently prayed, *Lord, your Word says that you will condemn every tongue that rises up against us. So I need you to do something with all these flapping lips today.*

Twenty-one

Mattie sat comfortably in the witness chair answering Luke Watson's questions. Cassandra was barely able to stay in her seat when Mattie told the judge that JT treats the children differently. That he separates them from each other. Mattie went so far as to tell the judge that when she offered to watch Lily, JT told her that Lily didn't need the special attention and love that a grandmother could give.

JT leaned over to Tom and said, "That's not true. She refused to watch Lily. She kept calling her illegitimate."

Cassandra glared at her mother as she heard the attorney ask, "And how does your daughter treat her two young sons?"

"Oh, like gold. There's not a thing those boys want that Cassandra don't see that they get it," Mattie said.

"And how does she treat Lily," Luke asked.

"Now that's a different story," Mattie said with a sad expression on her face.

"How different," Luke wanted to know.

"Well, I've seen her leave Lily in wet diapers for hours. And if Lily cries too long, Cassandra has slapped that poor little baby on them fat legs of hers."

"That's a lie," Cassandra said as she bounded out of her seat.

JT pulled her back down and whispered in her ear. "Calm down, Sanni. This is what they want you to do."

She heard JT, and she understood exactly why he wanted her to calm down, but that was her mother on that witness stand. She knew her mother didn't want her to be a mother to Lily, but Cassandra never imagined that she would lie to get Lily away from them.

Luke asked, "Why do you think your daughter treats Lily in this manner if she is such a good mother to her two boys?"

"You see, it's like this," Mattie began. "Cassandra is a good person, but you can only take so much from a cheat around, no good husband like the one she's got. She has told JT time and time again that he has to take care of Lily. But he's too busy running after other women to come home and see about his own child."

"In your opinion, who would be the better mother to Lily? Mrs. Diane Benson or your daughter, Cassandra Thomas?"

Mattie looked as if she were mulling the question over, and then said, "Diane might be trash, but she's Lily's mother. And while Cassandra may be a good person, she shouldn't have to raise another woman's child. That's how children get mistreated and end up dead."

Cassandra exploded. She jumped from her seat and started screaming at Mattie. "How could you? How could you? I will never forgive you. Do you hear me? I am done with you. I don't even know who you are."

JT tried to put Cassandra back in her seat, but there was no doing. She was outraged and would not be denied this tirade.

The bailiff and security guard grabbed Cassandra as the judge said, "That's it, ma'am. You're out of here."

"Take your hands off my wife," JT said as he grabbed Cassandra, pulling her away from the security guard.

"Why is she doing this? Why?" Cassandra screamed as she started gasping for breath.

"Don't panic, Sanni," JT said as he held onto her.

"Sir, we need you to let her go, or we'll have to remove both of you," the bailiff told JT.

"She's having a panic attack. Leave us alone!" JT yelled at the bailiff.

Tom grabbed JT and said in a low voice, "They're not going to hurt her, JT. They're just going to give her a seat out in the hall. Please sit back down, so you won't get thrown out as well."

"I can't leave her like this. She's struggling to breathe."

The judge brought the gavel down and said, "Ten minute recess."

JT sat Cassandra down and whispered in her ear, "Remember what I told you, Sanni. You can conquer this. Just trust God."

She leaned her head down between her legs and tried to calm herself. "Lord . . . help . . . me," Cassandra said between breaths. She knew people were staring at her, but she couldn't help herself.

"What's wrong with her?" Mattie asked as she walked past them.

"What do you care?" JT answered Mattie with scorn in his eyes.

"I care. I'm her mother." Mattie walked to the side of the table closest to Cassandra and started calling her name. "Cassandra, Cassandra!"

Her breathing was normalizing. Cassandra lifted her head, stared at her mother with contempt as she said, "Get away from me!"

The bailiff stepped up and told JT, "Your wife needs to leave the courtroom. If you won't let me take her out, both of you need to go."

JT stood up and started gathering his note pad and pieces of paper he'd scribbled notes on.

Cassandra grabbed JT's arm. She was ashamed of the way she had freaked out. She knew that at least one of them needed to remain in the courtroom and fight for Lily. Tears were streaming down her face, but she managed to say, "Sit back down, JT."

With his papers in his briefcase, he grabbed Cassandra's hand and stood her up. "Come on, Sanni, Tom can handle this without us for today."

She snatched her hand out of his. "No, JT. You stay here and fight for our baby."

"Are you sure, Sanni? I don't want you by yourself while you're this upset."

Cassandra regained as much of her composure as possible and then said, "I'll be all right. Lily needs you more than I do right now."

Mattie was still standing by Cassandra's side. She put her hand on her daughter's shoulder and asked, "Do you need me to sit with you?"

"I want you to get away from me." Cassandra removed her mother's hand from her shoulder and walked out of the courtroom without looking back.

As Tom got up for the cross-examination, JT could tell that Mattie had been shaken by Cassandra's outburst. But she recovered well enough by the time Tom asked his first question. "So, Ms. Daniels, you don't like your son-in-law very much do you?"

"Nope," she answered without giving it a second thought.

"Why not?" Tom prodded.

"For one thing, he's a dirty no good cheat. I didn't like him way before he started pushing up on all the sisters in church."

"Well then, what basis did you have for not liking your son-in-law if he hadn't done anything wrong yet?" Tom asked.

Mattie hunched her shoulders as if the logic of the matter didn't much concern her. "I got a problem with a lot of people, some I don't even know. I just didn't like him. Simple as that. He ended up proving me right."

"Have these *problems*," he did air quotation marks, and then continued, "that you have with a lot of people ever caused you to get on a witness stand and lie?"

"I don't know what you're talking about," Mattie said defiantly.

Tom pointed toward the exit and said, "Your daughter is distraught. She has been removed from this room with tear filled eyes because of the lies you just told."

Mattie folded her arms against her chest. "Cassandra will be all right."

"How, when you've just accused her of mistreating a child that she loves with all her heart?" Tom demanded to know.

"She shouldn't have to mother a child that's not hers," Mattie mumbled.

JT thought the worst was over after Mattie got off the stand, but Diane wasn't through with them. Her attorney brought out the pictures she'd taken of Cassandra at lunch with her therapist and accused Cassandra of running around on JT. Mattie was still sitting in the audience when Diane's attorney started passing around those pictures. She jumped out of her seat, outraged this time. "That's a lie! My daughter ain't never cheated on that man. And y'all not gon' lie on her like that."

The judge gave Mattie a scornful look and said, "Ma'am, you're here as a witness for the defense. Please sit back down."

"Not anymore, I'm not. Y'all got me twisted, bent, and all broke up if you think I'm gon' stay in here listening to this bunch of bull." She grabbed her purse and strutted out of the courtroom.

JT saw her rub her jaw as if it ached, and wondered if just because he thought about slapping the taste out of her mouth, God had actually done it for him. JT hoped so. And he willed his mind to slap her again.

By the end of that day's hearing, JT knew that they were in trouble. Tom tried to reassure him by saying, "Tomorrow's another day, man. They may have lied in here today, but we've got the truth on our side."

JT hoped that the truth would be enough. He found Cassandra and walked to her car with her. "Give me the keys. I'm going to drive you home."

"What about your car?" Cassandra asked.

"My car is still at work. I rode here with Tom."

She took the keys out of her purse and handed them to JT. "Thanks, I didn't feel much like driving."

As JT drove off, Cassandra asked him, "What happened to make my mother storm out of the courtroom?"

"You saw her leave?"

"Yeah."

"You didn't talk to her?"

A look of anger clung to Cassandra's eyes as she swore, "I will never speak to that woman again. But that doesn't mean I don't want to know what happened. So spill it."

JT glanced at his wife. She looked so distraught, he didn't know how much more she would be able to take, but he didn't want to lie to her. He was still working on restoring the trust she'd once had in him, so if he lied, even to protect her, Cassandra's faith in him might be shaken again. "You were right when you told me that Diane was going to use those pictures of you and your therapist against us. Her attorney showed those photos after your mother got off the stand, and he accused you of being too busy having an affair to take care of Lily."

The tears started falling again. Cassandra leaned against JT's arms and said, "We're going to lose our baby."

"No we're not, Sanni. Don't say that."

"It's true."

"It looks bad. I agree with you on that. But we have to trust God."

She opened the glove compartment, took out some tissue and blew her nose. "My own mother put the nail in our coffin. How could she do that?"

JT wished he had an answer for Cassandra. But the only thing that came to him was that Mattie did what she did simply because she had the devil in her. But did he really want to tell his wife that he thought her mother was pure evil?

They picked up the kids and went home. The rest of the evening, JT noticed that Cassandra held onto Lily a little longer than usual. She would change her diaper and then, instead of sitting her back down with the boys, Cassandra would rock Lily in her arms and kiss her forehead before putting her down. If Lily cried for any reason, Cassandra ran to her, picked her up, and held her so tight that Lily cried to be put back down.

JT ached for his wife. It was as if with each hug, Cassandra was fighting against her mother's lies. After the third attempt to cater to Lily's every whim, he sat Cassandra down and asked her, "What are you doing?"

"Nothing," she said, oblivious to her own actions.

"You haven't spent anytime with the boys since we got

home. They're going to start wondering why you're only holding Lily."

Tears bubbled in her eyes as she said, "My mother accused me of neglecting Lily, now you're accusing me of neglecting the boys?"

He wanted to tell her that nobody with any sense believed a word her mother said, but he knew his words would not take away the pain she was feeling from her mother's betrayal. So he left it alone and let her do what she needed to in order to get through the evening.

As he and Cassandra were putting the kids to bed, Bishop called. "What's up, Bishop? I'm helping Cassandra get the kids ready for bed so I can't talk long."

"I'm not going to keep you. I just thought you should know that I received a subpoena today."

"What? She subpoenaed you to our custody hearing too?"

Cassandra came running out of the boys' room and into their bedroom where JT was on the phone. "Who else did she subpoena?"

"I didn't get a subpoena for your custody hearing. This one is about you manipulating her into having sex," Bishop responded.

"I did not!"

"You didn't what? And who else has been subpoenaed?" Cassandra asked as she stood beside JT looking anxious.

He turned to his wife. "Bishop received a subpoena. It's not for the custody case though." JT couldn't bring himself to name the other case just then. But he saw from the look in Cassandra's eyes that she understood.

"Oh." She turned around and walked back out of the room.

"You're going to have to learn how to speak low so Cassandra doesn't hear everything you say," Bishop said.

JT rolled his eyes. "I've kept enough secrets from Cassandra, Bishop. I'm tired of hiding from the truth."

"And I guess you think telling the truth is going to smooth things over with you and Cassandra? How do you think she's going to feel when she hears about that deposition you just gave?"

"I don't think she wanted to hear something like that from me, but I already confessed everything to Cassandra. The way I see it, if my marriage is going to work, it's not going to be because I lied my way back into Cassandra's good graces."

"Well, if you want my opinion, you're going about this all wrong. You've tied the church's hands. I don't know how in the world we are going to be able to help you with a confession like that on record," Bishop said.

"I'm sorry if my confession puts the church in a bad light, Bishop. But I can't turn back now. That's what happened. I wish it hadn't, but it did."

"All right then, my boy. I have to come to town next week so our lawyers can help me work on my statements, so I guess I'll see you then."

"Okay, Bishop, I'll talk to you soon," JT said, and then hung up the phone.

That night when they went to bed, Cassandra asked JT, "Why do you suppose my father hasn't admitted to what he did to my mother?"

"I don't know, baby. Maybe he's ashamed of what happened, and can't deal with it himself, let alone admit it to other people."

"Maybe he's worried about losing his nice cushy bishop title. Maybe he'd rather be called bishop than father by someone like me."

They were facing each other as they lay in bed talking, but

that comment made JT sit up. "What do you mean, *someone like you?* What's wrong with you?"

"Parents don't always love their children like they're supposed to. Look at how my mother treated me today. That was not love and nobody can convince me of anything different."

"Your mother has issues, but I think what happened today had more to do with her hatred of me than her lack of love for you."

"Okay, then what about my father? He won't even claim me. He's always been a good father to his other children. So something must be wrong with me."

"I'm not going to let you do this to yourself, Sanni. You are the most lovable person I know. I did you wrong, your mother did you wrong, and yes; your father is wronging you by not telling the world that you are his. But none of this is a judgment against you." He pulled his wife into his arms and continued. "We have a whole lot of repenting to do, Sanni, but not you."

And like a river, the tears flowed as she held onto JT. Every so often he would whisper in her ear, "It's going to be okay, Sanni. I promise you, it will be better in the morning."

Late into the night, she curled up against him and went to sleep as he promised her yet again that things would be better in the morning. But unfortunately, by morning, things got worse.

Twenty-two

The phone rang at seven in the morning. Because of the fitful night's sleep he and Cassandra had, JT was tempted not to answer it. But he turned over and stretched out his arm to pick up the phone anyway. "Hello," he said groggily.

"Is this Cassandra's house?" the woman on the other end asked.

JT rubbed his eyes. "Yeah, but she's sleep."

"I wouldn't have called so early, but Mattie had a heart attack."

"What? Who is this?" JT asked as he sat up in bed.

"This is Joyce, Mattie's neighbor. I called the ambulance for her. And Mattie told me to call Cassandra. She was mumbling something, but all I could make out was *sorry*."

"Okay, I'll tell her. Thanks so much for calling." JT hung up and nudged Cassandra.

She hit his hand and mumbled, "Five more minutes."

"Cassandra, get up, honey," he said as he nudged her again.

She tossed and turned, and then finally laid on her back looking up at him. "What's so important it can't wait a few more minutes?"

"It's your mother, Sanni."

"Was that her on the phone? You should have hung up in her face. I told you I'm not talking to that woman again in life."

"Sanni, don't say that." He rubbed her arm trying to figure out how to comfort her.

Cassandra sat up. She wiped the sleep from her eyes and asked, "What's wrong, baby?"

She was calling him baby again. And all it took was for her mother to betray her. "It's your mom. She's in the hospital, honey. She had a heart attack this morning."

"What?" Cassandra asked, looking at him as if he'd just spoken in tongues and she was waiting on the interpretation.

"We need to go to the hospital. You get dressed, and I'll take care of the children." JT jumped out of bed and headed toward their bedroom door.

"JT?"

JT stopped and turned back to face his wife. The look on her face was horror stricken.

"Is my mom dead?"

JT tried to remember what Joyce had said. Something about the ambulance and the hospital. He didn't think she would have said it like that if Mattie had died before the ambulance got to her. "No, baby, I don't think so. Let's just get our clothes on and go find out what's going on. Okay?"

Cassandra got out of bed and the two of them ran around the house getting everybody ready to leave. JT called Ms. Shirley and asked if she could watch the children for a little while. She said she could, so they dropped the kids off and headed to the hospital.

"Why does her face look like that?" Cassandra demanded once she and JT were in the room Mattie had been placed in.

"That's from the stroke," the nurse said matter-of-factly.

"What stroke?" Cassandra asked with tears flooding her eyes.

JT stepped closer to Cassandra and pulled her into his arms. He told the nurse, "We were told that she had a heart attack."

The nurse had Mattie's chart in her hand, but she didn't need to look at it. "I was on duty when she arrived. She had been brought in because of a heart attack, but suffered a stroke upon arrival."

Mattie's eyes were closed and her lips twisted upward on the left side of her face as though rigor mortise had set in. Cassandra clung to JT as she said, "She looks like she's dead."

This time the nurse had compassion in her voice when she spoke. "Oh no, ma'am. The good thing about it is that she had the stroke while she was here. We were able to stop it from going any further."

"See, baby, it's going to be all right," JT said soothingly.

Cassandra clung to her husband. "I didn't want her to die. I promise, I didn't."

"I know that, Sanni. Your mom knows that too."

"I-I told her I would never speak to her again. B-but I didn't want it to be this way."

"Calm down, Cassandra. This is not your fault." He looked toward the nurse and asked, "Can you bring two chairs in here so we can sit with Mattie, please?"

"I'll get those for you right now," the nurse said before leaving the room.

JT rubbed Cassandra's back and arms, trying to calm her down. He then grabbed some tissue and wiped her wet face. The nurse brought the chairs in the room and JT said, "Sit down, baby. You're not going to be any good to your mother if you don't calm down so you can think straight."

Cassandra broke free from JT's grasp and went back to her mother's bed. She stood over Mattie and said, "I'm sorry, Mama. I'm so sorry."

Mattie turned her head toward Cassandra and slightly ope-ned her eyes. She looked disoriented as she opened her mouth and spoke.

Cassandra turned to the nurse. "What did she say?"

The nurse stepped forward and Mattie opened her mouth and gibberish came out again. "The stroke has affected her speech." The nurse stood on the side of Mattie's bed. She looked down at Mattie and asked, "Can you hear me, Ms. Daniels?"

Mattie shook her head, but it was obvious that she'd heard the nurse.

The nurse stepped away from Mattie's bed and motioned for Cassandra and JT to step out of the room with her. When they were both in the hall with her she said, "She appears to be a little confused right now. Once she comes around, we will be able to work with her to see if she has lost any other capabilities."

"What's wrong with her speech?" Cassandra asked. She was dumbstruck at the fact that Mattie couldn't get simple words out of her mouth, but that she sounded like more of a baby than Lily. Then she remembered that she had prayed that God would confound the tongues of all the liars in the courtroom yesterday and she wanted to call that prayer back. *I didn't want this, Lord.*

"Depending on which side of the brain the stroke affects, stroke victims can lose their grasp on language, eye sight; they can have trouble walking or using their arms. It all depends on what part of the brain shuts down."

"Will she be able to talk again?" JT asked with concern in his voice.

"We will have a speech therapist work with her as soon as she's able to begin. Most likely she will regain some speech, but probably not all of it. I'm sorry," the nurse said as she tried to walk away.

Cassandra stopped her. "Wait a minute. What about her face?"

"I can't give you any guarantees. It might straighten out, but then again it might not. We won't know for sure for a few days."

"Okay," she said and tried not to break down.

JT pulled her into his arms again. She put her arms around him because it felt right; secure. She remembered him telling her that she belonged with him. He was finally making her believe it.

While JT and Cassandra were going through the most traumatic event of their life, Margie Milner was making a life changing decision as well. Her mother had come with her to the attorney's office. Today was the day she and Diane would hear JT's rebuttal to their lawsuit. She and her mom had been talking about this case for more than a week. Betty Milner had been trying to convince Margie to let go of her bitterness and forgive JT, but Margie could only think of one reason she would forgive JT; he'd have to ask for it.

And then it happened. Luke Watson informed her that JT admitted that he had manipulated her into having an affair with him. "He even goes on in his deposition to apologize for everything he did to you," Luke said.

Betty nudged her daughter. "See, baby, the Lord knows how to settle a matter better than any attorney I've ever met."

Diane sat up in her seat and said, "This is such great news. We've got him right where we want him now. Did he apologize to me also?"

"Ah, no," Luke said as he averted his eyes from Diane and looked back at the documents in front of him.

"What do you mean, no? He wronged me just as well as he wronged Margie. And since I'm the one that got stuck with a kid by him, I'd say he owes me two apologies."

Luke turned the page on the document he was reading. He looked back at Diane and said, "Mr. Thomas's deposition states that you approached him first. He also says that he told you several times that he wasn't interested, but you wouldn't take no for an answer. He admits to giving in to you, but says that he never manipulated you into anything."

"That's a lie," Diane said, but she had the decency to look embarrassed.

Luke continued. "Mr. Thomas also states that you had other lovers besides him. If that is true, I'm going to need to know more about that."

"I know you don't believe a word that liar has said. JT is the only man I have been with besides my husband, and he knows that."

"Okay, I just need to be sure. We don't want any surprises when we have so much riding on this case," Luke said.

"That's why I told you we need to go to the media. I guarantee you we will have the sympathy vote on our side," Diane said.

Margie raised her hand, trying to halt the conversation. "I told you before that I am not interested in putting my business on the six o'clock news."

Diane turned on Margie. "Of course you're not interested. JT basically gave you your money on a silver platter. You're probably still sleeping with him, and this is his little way of paying for your services."

Betty stood up. "You will not speak to my daughter like that," she told Diane.

"Look, lady, this doesn't even concern you. You shouldn't even be in here while we're discussing our case."

"I have the right to be anywhere my daughter wants me to be," Betty fired back.

Margie had been praying all day long that God would show her what to do. She'd told the Lord that the money didn't matter to her. All she really wanted was for JT to admit what he'd done to her. Evidently, the Lord had been listening, so what was she still doing here? Margie stood up with her mother and said, "No, Mother, Diane is right. You don't belong in here and neither do I. Let's go."

"What?" Diane wailed as she, too, stood to her feet. "You can't just leave like that. Luke has invested a great deal of time on us."

Margie turned to Luke and said, "I am sorry I wasted your time, Mr. Watson. I will find a way to pay for the hours you wasted on me. But I can't be a part of this anymore. My mother told me about a scripture in the Bible that says, *vengeance is mine, saith the Lord. I will repay.* It made me realize that I entered into this lawsuit for all the wrong reasons. And I just can't live my life full of bitterness. I've got to move on."

Luke stood up and shook Margie's hand. "I appreciate your openness. We may need to call you as a witness, but you don't owe me any money. So don't worry about it."

"Thank you, Mr. Watson," Betty said as she grabbed hold of Margie's arm and walked out of the office.

Twenty-three

Mattie stayed in the hospital for three weeks. Since Mattie couldn't speak well enough to let the nurses know if she needed anything, Cassandra thought she needed to spend the night at the hospital to help take care of her mother. She stayed home with the kids while JT went to work. When he arrived home, Cassandra would leave him with the kids and go to the hospital for the night. But she had to admit, JT got the better end of the deal. The kids were all sleeping through the night, so he, at least, got a good night's sleep. On the other hand, when Cassandra wasn't being awakened by her mother's moans and groans, the nurses were coming into the room to check Mattie's vital signs, temperature, and whatever else they could think to do between midnight and seven in the morning.

Her mother was improving. Her face had straightened itself out, she had full use of both arms and she was walking with a cane. By the second week of hospitalization, although Mattie was improving, Cassandra was worn out. Then one evening JT approached her as she was packing her overnight bag. He told her, "You're not going to the hospital tonight."

She grabbed her toothbrush and face cleanser out of the medicine cabinet as she said, "I have to, JT. Last night I hit the nurse button and it took them twenty minutes to get to her room. What if it had been an emergency? She needs someone there with her."

"Yeah, she needs someone to be there. But not you; not tonight."

She turned around getting ready to face off with JT for being selfish. Cassandra was an only child, so who did he think was going to stay with Mattie if she didn't? Just as she was getting ready to let him have it, she noticed that he had his pillow in his hand and then he reached around her and grabbed his toothbrush out of the medicine cabinet. "What are you doing?"

"I'm going to the hospital tonight."

Her brow rose as she asked, "You're going to do what?"

"I can see that you're worn out. So I'm taking my turn."

Dumbfounded by this act of kindness, Cassandra opened her mouth and put her foot in it before she could stop herself. "But you don't even like my mother."

JT took the overnight bag from Cassandra. He took her stuff out of it and laid it on the bed, then put his toiletries in it as he said, "I've been praying about this, and the way I see it, this whole situation is really quiet simple. You love your mother, and I love you. So I've decided to make her love me like the son she never had."

Cassandra didn't want to hurt JT's feelings, but she didn't think that would ever happen. However, she didn't want him to give up on treating her mother respectfully either, so she asked, "What if that never happens?"

JT smiled and hunched his shoulders. "Then I'm going to love her anyway."

Cassandra went to him then. She wrapped her arms around him and said, "Thank you."

He held her tightly and said, "I got this, Sanni. Don't worry about a thing. Your mom won't be able to resist me for much longer."

By the time JT got home from work the next day, his eyes were blood shot. So Cassandra knew that the nurses had given him the same treatment she'd been receiving. But he'd gone back three days later anyway. At that moment, even with lawsuits and custody battles looming over their heads, Cassandra didn't think she would trade JT Thomas for anyone.

The judge had given them a continuance on both cases. Now that Mattie was out of the hospital and living with Cassandra and JT, all of it was about to start up again. But Cassandra was too busy working with speech, physical, and occupational therapists to stress out over things she couldn't control. She told herself that their lives were in God's hands even as she set about adjusting their lives to accommodate her mother's new reality.

Cassandra didn't want her mother trying to go up the stairs, so she removed the couch from the family room and had Mattie's bedroom furniture put in there. She knew the new décor wouldn't win her any prizes on *Rate My Space*, one of the shows she enjoyed watching on *HGTV*. But this was what her mother needed, and Cassandra was determined to do everything she could to nurse her mother back to health.

She was still feeling guilty about praying that God would confound the tongues of the liars that were in the courtroom that day. And now her mother couldn't speak. The speech therapist had been working with her, but so far, all Mattie was able to do was say her own name and Cassandra's. She couldn't get the whole name out though, so now instead of calling her Cassandra, her mother called her Sanni like JT. That was okay with Cassandra, but when Mattie would try to tell her something, and the whole sentence would come out like gibberish, that broke her heart. She wanted so desperately to have a two way conversation with her mother. She would even listen to any joke Mattie wanted to tell.

It was times like this when Cassandra wished she had some girlfriends. She'd never been much for hanging out with a bunch of women. That whole scene was too catty for her taste. But while JT was at work and her mother lay in bed sleeping, it would be so nice to be able to pick up the phone and tell a friend about the things she was going through. When she was at the grocery store yesterday, she bumped into Ellen Peoples. Cassandra hadn't seen her at church the last few Sundays, but she thought she was a nice lady, so she invited her and her husband to dinner Saturday evening.

She'd forgotten to tell JT, but he didn't have to cook the meal anyway. She looked at her watch and realized that she had two hours before her guests arrived. JT would be home in about an hour. He had taken the kids to the airport with him. Even though they had a lot on their hands, JT was excited to finally be able to bring Lamont home.

The couch that had been in the family room had a bed inside it. Since Cassandra had already put the couch and chair in the basement, they'd agreed that Lamont would stay down there. JT picked up an extra TV from Mattie's house and put it in the basement. Now all Cassandra had to do was prepare dinner.

It was going to be a pasta night. Penne noodles with shrimp, chicken, and alfredo sauce. She couldn't put the shrimp or chicken in her mom's portion though. Mattie's food had to be pureed because she was having trouble swallowing food that wasn't crushed up. Cassandra put the noodles on to boil and went back in the family room to check on Mattie. She was still sleeping, so Cassandra went back into the kitchen and put the chicken and shrimp on the stove. She had cooked this meal numerous times because JT loved it. He also liked salad, garlic bread, and broccoli as side dishes. So she fixed all of it. He had done so much for her mother these last few weeks that Cassandra looked for things to do for him. They'd even made love again. That is, when she didn't fall into bed dead tired from taking care of the kids and her mother.

The door bell rang, Cassandra looked at her watch. It was ten before six and JT still hadn't gotten back home yet. She ran to the door and opened it. Ellen Peoples was standing there with a bottle of red wine in her hands. She handed it to Cassandra. "I hope red is okay. I didn't know what you were fixing for dinner."

"Thank you, but we don't drink," Cassandra said as she handed the bottle back to Ellen. "We have iced tea and lemonade. I hope either of those will be okay with you."

"That's fine," Ellen said as she strutted in the house in her three-inch heels, tight fitting jeans, and low cut blouse.

Cassandra looked toward their drive way, and then asked, "Are you and your husband driving separate cars?"

"He had to work."

"Oh, I wish you had told me. We could have planned our dinner for another time. I think JT would really enjoy connecting with Eric."

"I started to call when I found out. But I really needed to get out of the house. So I decided to come by myself. I hope that's not a problem."

Cassandra watched Ellen sit down on the couch in the living room. To her horror, she noticed that Ellen's breasts were even more exposed when she sat down. Cassandra wanted to hand her a jacket to cover up with, like the old mothers at church handed out embroidered handkerchiefs to women sitting on the front pew with short dresses on. "No, it's not a problem. I'm sure JT will have plenty of time to get to know Eric." She pointed toward the back of the house. "I'm going to call JT and find out what's keeping him, and then I'll get my mom up so we can all have a little chat before dinner."

Ellen crossed her legs and leaned back on the sofa. "Don't worry about me. I know how to make myself comfortable."

Cassandra was getting a bad feeling about having a stylish and overly exposed woman like Ellen in her home. But then she reprimanded herself. Either she trusted JT or she didn't. She picked up the phone in the kitchen and called him. When JT picked up, she said, "Where are you?"

"Around the corner. I should be home in less than two minutes. What's up?"

"Did Lamont's plane get in late or something?"

"No, I took the kids to the park and for some ice cream after I picked Lamont up."

Cassandra laughed. "You're not slick, JT. I know that you're just trying to tire them out so they won't have me running back and forth all night long."

"Hey, whatever works."

"Okay, just hurry up. We have company," she told him as she hung up the phone. Cassandra opened the fridge and took the pitcher of iced tea out. She poured the tea in a glass and took it into the living room and handed it to Ellen. "JT should be here any minute. I'm going to get my mother up so she can sit in the living room with us for a little while. I'll be right back."

JT pulled up in the driveway. He and Lamont got out of the car. Then Lamont helped him get the kids out. Jerome and Aaron ran toward the front door while JT carried Lily. "Slow down, boys. The house isn't going anywhere."

"Open the door, Dad. Come on. I want to show Mommy the cut I got when I fell off the swing," Jerome told him.

JT didn't know if he wanted Jerome to rush in the house and show Cassandra his boo boo. He would probably end up in the dog house because his son thought his name was Geronimo rather than Jerome. He opened the door while trying to think of the best way to tell Cassandra that boys will be boys, and accidents happened. But then he saw Ellen Peoples with her legs crossed, leaning back on his couch sipping juice from his cup and he lost his cool. "What are you doing in my house?"

"Well, hello to you too, Pastor," Ellen said as she put the glass down on the coffee table."

Lamont had his bags in his hand. He nudged JT and asked, "Where do you want me to put these?"

JT pointed toward the kitchen. "The door to the basement is in the kitchen. And don't worry, I know it's tight quarters here right now. But we should be able to find you your own place in no time."

"Cool," Lamont said as he gazed quizzically in the woman's direction, but didn't say anything. He just headed in the direction of the basement.

JT turned back toward Ellen and said, "I want you to get up and get out of my house this instant."

"JT, what has gotten into you?" Cassandra asked as she rounded the corner with Mattie holding onto her shoulder while she carried her mother's cane.

JT turned to Cassandra. He didn't know what to say. He felt as if he was caught, but he hadn't done anything wrong.

Cassandra helped her mother sit down on the couch, then she told JT. "I invited Ellen over for dinner. Are you really that mad because she and her husband have found another church to attend?"

"No. I'm the one that asked her to find some place else to attend."

"Why on earth would you do that?" Cassandra was still holding Mattie's cane. She pointed it at JT and said, "Didn't I tell you that we need all the members we can get."

"We don't need this member, Cassandra," JT said flatly.

Ellen stood up and approached the door. "Well, look, I can tell when I'm not wanted. So I'll just be on my way." She brushed against JT and said, "One day you'll realize what you're missing out on and come get it."

"I've got everything I need already," he said as he stepped away from her.

With an angry brow raised, Cassandra asked, "What did you say to my husband?"

Ellen turned around with her hand on her hip. "Oh, Cassandra. I forgot you were standing there. Thanks for the iced tea, but I would rather have JT."

Cassandra raised the cane like a weapon and aimed for Ellen's head. Ellen ran through the door that JT had left open and Cassandra tried to follow her, but JT grabbed her. "Just let her go."

Cassandra snatched her arm out of JT's grasp as she told him, "You can go with her."

His eyes bugged out. "I didn't do anything."

"You didn't do anything," Cassandra repeated as she lifted the cane again. She hit at JT but he grabbed the cane and wrestled it out of her hand.

He held Cassandra close as he tried to explain. "Listen to me. I didn't do anything with that woman."

"Let me go, JT."

He released her, but kept talking. "She came to my office a few weeks back claiming that she left her Bible in the auditorium. When I told her that we didn't find any Bibles, she told me that she really wanted to talk to me. She basically let me know that she wanted to have an affair."

"This is just unbelievable, JT. Why would Ellen come onto you like that?"

"Baby, I have no idea why people do the things they do, but it happened. And I told her I wasn't interested and asked that she find another church to attend."

A sound behind them caused Cassandra and JT to turn around. Mattie was laughing. Cassandra pointed toward her mother as she said, "I haven't heard her laugh since she had the stroke."

JT said, "She's laughing at me." He then tried to plead his case to his mother-in-law. "I didn't do anything, Mattie."

Mattie held out her hands and rubbed her fingers together like she did when she wanted to write something down.

"You want some paper?" Cassandra asked.

Mattie nodded.

Cassandra went back into the family room/bedroom and grabbed the pad and pen Mattie used to communicate with them. She handed them to her mother and stood back.

Mattie wrote on the pad and then turned it around so Cassandra and JT could see what she wanted them to know. *Diane's friend.*

"Who's Diane's friend, Mama?"

Mattie pointed to the door Ellen had just escaped through.

"Ellen? Are you saying that Ellen is Diane's friend?" Cassandra asked.

Mattie nodded again.

"I knew it!" JT declared. "I knew I recognized that woman from somewhere. I must have seen her with Diane or something."

"So," Cassandra said. Turning back toward her husband, anger still etched across her face.

"Don't you get it, Sanni. Diane tried to set me up. I should have recognized it right off. The woman acted just like Diane did when she . . ." he let his statement trail off. He and Cassandra weren't cool enough to have that kind of discussion.

"I am so tired of this," Cassandra said, her hands balling into fists.

"But I didn't do anything." He pointed to Mattie and said, "Even Mattie can see that. Right?" he asked as he turned to his mother-in-law.

She nodded, backing JT up, and even though it shocked him, he trodded on as if Mattie taking his side in anything was a normal occurrence. "Baby, I didn't ask that woman to come to my office, and I didn't ask Diane to try to set me up."

"I don't care, JT. I'm sick of all these tricks and lawsuits and everything else. I want this to be over. And you better make it happen fast, or I'm out of here," she said as she punched him in the shoulder, and then went upstairs and slammed their bedroom door.

There goes my happy night, he thought. She hadn't even noticed Jerome's boo-boo, but he was still in the dog house.

Twenty-four

On Sundays a home healthcare nurse came to the house to sit with Mattie so the family could go to church. Lamont had decided to attend church with them. Since there wasn't enough room in JT's car for all three kids, Cassandra, and Lamont, Cassandra said she would drive her own car this morning. But as far as JT could tell, she wasn't all that unhappy about not having to ride with her husband to church.

Evidently, Lamont noticed it too, because when he got in the car, he asked, "So what's going on with you and Cassandra?"

"She's upset with me right now, but we'll get through it," JT told Lamont as he drove down the street.

"It's not about that woman who was at the house last night, is it? You're not cheating again, are you?"

The tone of Lamont's voice was angry. But JT knew the young man wasn't angry with him; more like scared. Lamont had left the only life he knew solely based on JT's word that things would get better for him. If he thought that JT really hadn't changed, that nothing had gotten better in JT's life, then where was his hope?

"No, Lamont, I'm not cheating with that woman." JT answered. "A lot of things have happened since I turned my life back over to God, but I trust the Lord and believe Cassandra and I will come through all of this better than we went into it."

"Okay, man. I just wanted to make sure because I could hang with jackleg preachers in my own hometown. You know what I mean?"

Yeah, JT knew exactly what he meant. Lamont was finally looking to make a change in his life and wasn't trying to be hindered by anyone else's foolishness. That brought a smile to JT's face. "I'm glad you came, Lamont," was all JT said as he pulled the car up to the youth center. He waited on Cassandra to pull into the lot, and then they got out of the car and helped her with the children.

"Thanks, Lamont," Cassandra said as Lamont helped Jerome out of his seat. She walked past JT without saying a word.

Lamont looked back at JT and said, "I guess you done lost your amen corner today, huh?"

"Shut up, boy," JT said as he walked into the auditorium, trying to catch up with Cassandra so he could give Aaron to her.

Despite Cassandra's frosty attitude, service went well. There were several new faces in the crowd. If this keeps up, JT thought to himself, they would soon be able to get their own building. After he'd finished preaching, JT noticed that Cassandra stayed seated and didn't bother about greeting the new people. He knew she was gun shy after that stunt Ellen pulled. But JT couldn't have that. He enjoyed watching Cassandra talk visitors into coming back to their church. He pulled her up from her seat and walked over to a couple as they were leaving the auditorium.

"Thank you so much for coming," JT said as he shook hands with the man, and then his wife. He nodded in Cassandra's direction. "This is my wife, Cassandra."

The man said, "I'm Jarrod, and this is my wife Serena. We're new in town and just checking out the local churches."

This was normally where Cassandra started gushing about

JT's preaching and how she wished the visitor would come back, but she didn't say anything, so JT told them, "Well, I hope this won't be your last visit to our little church."

Serena brightened as she said, "Oh no, Pastor Thomas. We intend to come back. Your message today hit us right where we live. I can tell you are anointed of God."

Cassandra rolled her eyes as she said, "Pastor Thomas has a wife to tell him how wonderfully he preaches, but thank you for visiting with us." She turned and walked away from them without saying another word.

"Did I say something wrong?" Serena asked as she watched Cassandra walk away.

Jarrod pulled his wife a little closer to him, and protectively planted a kiss on her forehead.

"No, Sister Serena, you didn't do anything wrong at all. If the two of you keep visiting with us, I just might tell you our story. Then you'll understand why my wife seems a little standoffish at times."

Jarrod shook JT's hand again as he told him, "If you don't mind me saying so, Pastor, we've heard your story. It was the reason Serena and I decided to attend church here."

Serena smiled, but JT now recognized the lingering pain in her eyes.

"I understand what your wife is going through, and I will keep her lifted in prayer. You can count on that, Pastor Thomas." And then with a small giggle, Serena added, "But just so you know, I won't be praising your sermons anymore."

JT laughed with her. "Fair enough. But thank you for praying for my wife. I appreciate that."

"Keep your head up, Pastor; a brighter day is coming," Jarrod assured him as the three parted company.

JT kept shaking hands and passing along friendly greetings

until Lamont strolled up to him and said, "Cassandra's leaving."

He turned to see his wife struggling with the three children. He excused himself from the man he was holding a conversation with and ran over to Cassandra. "Let me help you put the kids in the car."

"Did I ask you to help me with the kids?" Cassandra snapped

Cassandra had Lily on one hip and Aaron on the other, while trying to hold Jerome's hand. JT took Lily and grabbed Jerome's hand. "It looked like you needed me," he said as he walked toward her car.

"The thing I need you to do, you've refused. So why should I keep asking you to do stuff for me?"

JT opened the car door and let Jerome climb into his seat while he put Lily in her car seat. When Cassandra leaned into the backseat to put Aaron in his car seat, JT said, "Why do you keep arguing with me over something that I have no control over?"

"You have control over this. The money is sitting right in our account."

"Here we go with this again," JT said as he shut the rear passenger door and walked over to Cassandra's side of the car. "That money belongs to Lamont, and even if I borrowed it to give to Diane; she'd just keep coming back for more. We need to let this play out in the court system and put our faith in God."

The look of anger on Cassandra's face and the way she got in the car and slammed the door without saying a mumbling word to him, made JT wish for that brighter day Jarrod had just told him about.

***

Cassandra had had enough. She hated that she was upset with JT, because she really did believe he was a changed man. But this lawsuit hanging over their heads and the thought of losing Lily was too much for her. She wasn't just thinking about herself right now. Her children would be hurt if knowledge of this lawsuit got out. And if they lost the custody case, she and JT would lose Lily. She just couldn't sit back and let that happen.

She was supposed to turn right at the stop light to go home, but at the last minute Cassandra changed her mind and turned left. She knew where Diane and Joe lived, and she intended to drive over there and confront that horrible woman once and for all. JT could wait on God if he wanted, but she was going to resolve this whole mess today.

She pulled into Diane's driveway, got out of the car, and rang the doorbell. She then went back to her car and reached her hand into the car and honked the horn three times. She looked in the backseat and saw that the kids were sleep, so she took her hand off the horn, leaned against the car, and waited for someone to open the front door.

"Have you lost your mind?" Diane said as she stormed down the stairs.

Joe came out behind her and tried to pull Diane back in the house. "Go back in the house, Diane. I'll talk to Cassandra."

Diane laughed in his face. "Do you think she came over here to see you?"

"No, but I don't think it's a good idea for you two to talk. Just let me handle this," Joe said.

"Go back in the house, Joe. I thought you were going to fix the kids something to eat," Diane said as she brushed his hand off her arm and strutted over to Cassandra. "Why would you come to my house making all this racket?"

"At least I waited until the afternoon. I remember a morning when you came to my house leaning on the doorbell, and then left us with a package."

Diane bent down and looked into the car. She then stood straight again and asked, "What? Are you bringing her back?"

"Not on your life. You don't deserve my daughter."

"How dare you stand in my face and claim to be the mother of a child I birthed."

"It takes more to be a mother than simply giving birth. I'm the one who holds Lily when she cries. I make sure that she's fed when she's hungry, and above all that, I love her like a mother."

Diane looked at Cassandra scornfully. "You're pathetic. What kind of woman wants to take care of another woman's brat?"

Cassandra didn't care what Diane thought of her. She had one objective in driving over there and she was going to handle her business. She put her finger in Diane's face and said, "Leave my family alone."

Diane folded her arms around her chest. "Your husband started with me. And you're probably the one who encouraged him to take me to court for custody of my child."

"You don't want Lily. You left her with us and never even called to check on her."

"That doesn't mean I want you to have custody of my child."

The look on Cassandra's face was that of disgust. "Look at you," she said to Diane. "You're standing within inches of Lily and you haven't tried to hold her. You've done little more than glance at her."

Diane looked in the backseat of the car again. She rolled

her eyes. "She's sleep. What do you want me to do, wake her up so she can see her real mommy?"

"No, I want you to leave us alone. And I'm willing to offer you a hundred thousand dollars to do it."

Diane laughed. "Why would I take a hundred thousand dollars from you? We're seeking five times that much in my lawsuit."

"Who do you think you're kidding, Diane? I know that Margie has dropped her name from the lawsuit. You're the only one left. And we both know that JT didn't manipulate you."

"You weren't there... you don't know what happened. But why doesn't it surprise me that you believe what JT said?"

Cassandra raised her hands, halting Diane's protests. "You know what, Diane? Save the theatrics for the courtroom. I'm only offering this money once. If you lose, don't think I'm going to give you the money anyway. So think carefully before refusing."

Diane tapped her front tooth with her fingernail as she pondered Cassandra's offer. When she stopped tapping she asked, "What do I have to do to get this money?"

"Drop your lawsuit against JT and give us sole custody of Lily," Cassandra answered matter-of-factly.

"You don't ask for much, do you?"

"Take it or leave it," Cassandra said as she opened the car door and got back in the driver's seat. "We both know that you don't have a case against JT without Margie. So give it up; take the money and run."

Diane didn't respond. She stood there tapping her finger against her tooth again.

Cassandra started the ignition, and then said, "What's it going to be? Once I leave here today, I won't offer you this money again."

Diane bent down and looked into the backseat at Lily again. "I might want to see her sometime. Will you allow that?"

"I don't know. I need to talk to JT about that."

Diane stood back up, shaking her head. "I can't just let my baby go like that. I mean, I might not want to be a full time mother right now, but that doesn't mean I don't ever want to see her."

Cassandra put the car in reverse. "I'm leaving. Get your money the best way you can."

Diane grabbed hold of the driver door. "Wait. Wait a minute." She looked at Lily again, and then asked, "When can I get the money?"

"I'll have the money tomorrow afternoon. You call me and let me know where you want to meet to pick it up." After saying that, Cassandra didn't wait for a response; she pulled out of the driveway and headed home. JT would forgive her. She was sure of it. She would leave Lamont with twenty-five thousand. That was enough for him to begin a new life. And the hundred thousand would help her and JT move on with their lives.

Twenty-five

On Monday morning, JT woke Lamont up and took him to the bank. The money he owed Lamont was causing a wedge between him and his wife, and he wanted it gone. Lamont opened a bank account, and then JT transferred the hundred and twenty-five thousand dollars into his account without batting an eye.

When they walked out of the bank, Lamont said, "I thought you weren't going to give me my money until I got my GED."

"Why didn't you remind me about that GED before we transferred the money?" JT said with a playful grin on his face. They got in the car, but before they took off, JT turned to Lamont and said, "Look, you're a grown man. You don't need me watching over your money anymore. I will say this though, a hundred and twenty-five thousand dollars may seem like a lot of money, but if you spend it unwisely, it'll be gone before you know it."

"Man, you don't have to worry about me. That near death experience helped me to see how I've just been wasting my life." He leaned back in the passenger seat and said, "I've got goals, and now I've got enough money to make it happen."

Smiling, JT said, "You can't just drop news like a brother having goals and not spill the beans. What's up?"

He stretched his legs out. "I don't know if I want to put my business in the street."

"Spill it."

Lamont looked hesitant, but then he leaned over and pulled his backpack from the backseat of JT's car. He unzipped it and said, "I listened to what you said about changing my environment and changing my life." He pulled a camera out of his backpack and continued, "All my friends thought this was stupid, so I kind of gave it up. But as I lay in the hospital bed thinking about what I wanted out of life, a picture of this camera kept flashing in my head."

"That's a pretty professional looking camera," JT said.

Lamont lifted and twisted the lens cap off. "It's the best. I spent twelve hundred dollars on this beauty. And she's worth every penny."

JT noticed how Lamont's eye lit up as he held that camera in his hand. He hadn't seen the boy this passionate about anything since they met.

"It's got high resolution, scene recognition, one-button live view—"

JT lifted a hand as he laughed, "Okay, you sold me. You know a little something about cameras. Are you telling me that you want to be a photographer or the person who makes those things?"

Lamont gave JT a duh-are-you-stupid look. "Now we both know I don't have the skills to make this camera. I don't even have my GED." He lifted the camera and took a few shots of JT while driving. "But I can take pictures like nobody's business. I paint too."

"How come I'm just finding this out?"

Lamont put the camera down. He stared out the window as they drove. "People don't understand. They think you're soft if you want to do stuff like this."

"So you're willing to let go of your dreams, worrying about what people think?"

"I had been willing. But a near death experience helps to put things in perspective. I'm going to get my GED, and then I'm going to college; majoring in art."

JT smiled. He might not have helped Lamont find his place in life as much as his motorcycle accident did, but he'd provided the money to fund his dreams, and that was good enough for him. "I think you should write to your father and let him know how you plan to use the money."

Lamont waved that suggestion off. "Naw, he won't think it's hard enough."

"Look, I'm not trying to put your dad down, but robbing people and going to prison on the regular; that ain't hard. Matter-of-fact, Jimmy picked the easy way out. Trying to live right and fighting for your dreams, now that's hard."

"That's not the kind of hard I'm talking about."

"I know that, but do you understand what I'm trying to tell you?"

"Yeah," Lamont said. He then leaned back in his seat and smiled contently. "I think I just might write the old man a letter after all. He needs to know that his ill-gotten gain is being put to good use."

"Where else would you like to go? I'll take you anywhere you want today. Tomorrow you'll be using the bus to get where you need to be."

"Oh. Well, if that's the case, take me to a car dealership. I got enough money to get my own wheels now."

"Okay, but you don't need to spend your money on a brand new car when you've got to stretch that money to get you through four years of college. So, I'm taking you to a used car dealership."

Lamont frowned. "Why you gotta always act like somebody's daddy?"

"I am three bodies' daddy. And you need a father figure to help you understand life. I've seen people lose way more money than you have and end up living on the streets."

"Forget all that nonsense you talking. I know what I'm doing."

JT didn't respond; he just kept driving. He pulled into Jay Pontiac Buick GMC. GM was closing some of its dealerships, so JT wanted to do his part in making sure that people bought American. They got out the car and walked around the lot. JT point out a black 2008 Chevy Impala. That, and a 2007 Buick LaCrosse. Both were selling for thirteen thousand, but Lamont wasn't interested.

He walked straight over to a 2008 white Cadillac Escalade that was selling for twenty-seven thousand. JT shook his head as he walked over to Lamont.

"I know what you're going to say, but I can really see myself in this car. I'm sure I can talk the dealer down to twenty-five thou." Lamont said while running his hand across the hood of the Escalade.

"Boy, with the taxes and fees that are going to be accessed, you'll still be spending thirty thou."

"I didn't think about the taxes," Lamont answered honestly.

JT's cell phone rang. He looked down and saw that it was Cassandra. He looked back at Lamont and said, "You better think about it." Then he stepped away from Lamont and pushed the talk button on his phone. "What's up, baby?" he said in his most seductive voice. He was determined to get the home fires burning again. He just didn't know what to do to make her happy these days, but he was still going try.

"Where's the money, JT?" Cassandra screamed through the phone.

"What money?"

"Don't play dumb with me. I'm at the bank, and the money is gone."

"That money wasn't ours, Sanni. I transferred it into Lamont's account this morning."

"I want it back right now. Do you hear me, JT. Get that money back, or I'm going home and packing me and the kids up."

"Why are you talking like this? You knew I was going to give the money to Lamont."

"That's it. I'm sick of everyone else coming before me and the kids. I'm not just going to sit by and watch Diane take Lily from us, when I know she doesn't care anything about her. We're leaving, JT." Cassandra hung the phone up.

JT was shocked. Had his wife really gone to the bank to steal Lamont's money? But then, hadn't he done the same thing to Jimmy after they'd lost Sarah and he'd stopped trusting God. He turned around and saw Lamont talking with a car salesman. JT rushed over to them and grabbed Lamont by the arm and said, "I've got to get home. I'll bring you back here tomorrow."

"Naw, JT, I want to drive that beauty off the lot today," Lamont told him.

The salesman stepped forward with a big grin on his face. "We can make that happen for you, young man. Just say the word."

JT turned to the man. "His money won't even be available in his account for three more days. Just give him your card, and we'll be back to see you in a couple of days." JT got behind the wheel of his car while Lamont took the business card from the eager salesman. Lamont was saying something to the salesman as he pointed at the Escalade. JT honked the horn.

Lamont jumped in the car. "What's up, man? Something wrong with one of the kids?"

"No, something's wrong with my wife," was all JT said as he drove home like a man about to lose everything that mattered.

Cassandra was frantic as she drove toward the house. She came to a red light and then hit the steering wheel with her fist. Tears were streaming down her face as she asked aloud, "How could JT do it? Why would he take that money now?" The money had been sitting in their account for five months, and neither one of them had touched it. But on the exact morning that she was to give that money to Diane, JT pulls it out of their account.

Her cell phone started ringing. Cassandra looked at the caller display and got a headache. Rolling her eyes, she pushed talk on her cell phone and kept driving. "Yeah, what is it?"

"You know what I'm calling about? Where do you want to meet?" Diane asked.

The fact that this woman was willing to give up her baby for money showed Cassandra just how unfit she was to parent a beautiful child like Lily. There was no way that she would ever turn Lily over to Diane Benson. "I'm on my way to the bank now. I'll give you a call after I get the money and we can make meet up then."

"Okay," Diane said and then hesitated a moment before saying, "Look, Cassandra, I know I have no right to ask, but I need you to do me a favor."

Cassandra scoffed, "You already slept with my husband, Diane. I'm all out of favors for you."

"It's just a small one. I just want you to bring Lily with you when you bring the money. If I'm going to give her up, I just want to hug her one last time. That's all."

Taken off guard by Diane's show of interest in Lily, Cassandra didn't know what to say. She pushed the END button on her cell phone and kept driving. She looked through the rearview mirror at Aaron and Lily as they sat in their car seats in the back of the car. Jerome had been sleep when she left home so she left him with her mom.

As Cassandra thought through her troubles, she realized that her mom was the reason for all the stress she was going through. If Mattie had not lied on her in court that day, she wouldn't be so worried about losing Lily. And if the judge believed what Mattie had said, what's to stop him from having children's services take Jerome and Aaron? "I'm not going to let them win," she promised Aaron and Lily as she glanced in the mirror again.

JT wanted to be noble. He was Mr. Do-The-Right-Thing at the wrong time. She would show him. She was going home to pack her children's clothes and get as far away from this town as possible. She loved JT and wanted to make their marriage work, but she couldn't do that if she lost her children because of his foolish behavior.

As she pulled up to the house she saw JT's car in the driveway. Good, she thought, *he can kiss his kids good-bye before we leave.*

Twenty-six

Perfect timing, JT thought as he turned off his car, and then watched as Cassandra pulled in the driveway behind him. As he and Lamont got out of the car, he could see that Aaron and Lily were in the car with Cassandra. He looked over at Lamont and said, "You grab Aaron and I'll get Lily."

The two quickly moved to the rear doors of Cassandra's four door sedan. They flung the doors open and both men grabbed a child.

Cassandra jumped out of the car screaming, "No, leave them alone. You don't care anything about us. Just leave my children alone."

JT had Lily on his hip. He turned to Cassandra and noticed that she had a crazed look in her eyes. He tried to speak calmly. "Come in the house with me so we can discuss this."

She put her hands on her hips as she defiantly stood in front of him. "Did you ask him to give us the money back?"

JT glanced at Lamont with a look of embarrassment on his face. He then turned back to his wife and said, "No, Sanni, I can't do that."

She reached for Lily. "Then give me my baby. We're getting out of here."

JT stepped away from her as he held Lily a little tighter. He began walking toward the house. Cassandra tried to pull Lily out of his arms, but only succeeded in making Lily cry.

"I'm sorry, baby. I wasn't trying to hurt you," she said as she turned her sights onto Lamont. "Give me my baby," she said as she charged into the house after Lamont.

JT shook his head as he handed Lily to Lamont as well. "Take the kids to the basement, man. I'll explain all this later."

Cassandra leaped toward Lamont like a lioness after her cub. But JT grabbed her arms and pulled her close to him. "Get off of me, JT."

Lamont was frozen in the front door. JT was holding Cassandra with both hands so he had to nudge Lamont with his shoulder. "Go on, man. And lock the door from the inside. I'll let you know when things are under control."

Lamont held the kids like they were footballs as he ran down the hallway toward the basement.

"Let go!" Cassandra struggled to get away, but it was no use, even in her current state of anger, JT was too powerful for her. She couldn't break free.

"I can't let you go, Sanni. Don't you know how much I need you?"

"We can't stay here, JT. Without that money everything is lost. Diane is going to take Lily. And because of the things my mother said about me, we might even lose Jerome and Aaron. Don't you see that I have to leave?"

"S-st-op!"

Cassandra and JT both heard the broken word and turned to see Mattie leaning against the wall in the hallway leading to the living room.

Mattie looked so frail, holding that cane and leaning against the wall for support with such a pained looked on her face. He was sure that she'd heard Cassandra accuse her of being the reason they might lose their children. Since he had just as much to do with it as the lies Mattie had told, he wanted to go over there, hug her, and let her know it would be all right. He released Cassandra's arms. And it was as if she and he were finally on the same page.

Cassandra walked over to Mattie, put her arms around her, and said, "I'm sorry, Mama. I shouldn't have said that."

Tears ran down Mattie's face as she attempted to talk again. But she sounded like a twelve-month-old child trying to form words.

"Let me help you back to your bed, Mama." Cassandra took the cane out of Mattie's hand and attempted to lock arms with her so she could walk her back to her bedroom.

But JT could tell that Mattie had expended all of her energy just walking to the living room. He picked her up and carried her back to bed, then gently pulled the covers up to her chest and fluffed her pillow to ensure that she was comfortable. "You need to rest, Mattie. Please don't get up again until your physical therapist comes this evening."

But Mattie had fear in her eyes as she pointed at Cassandra, who was standing behind JT. She then pointed at JT, and then mimicked loud talking by repetitively pressing her thumb against her fingers like a mouth opening and closing.

JT looked back toward Cassandra, and then turned back to his mother-in-law and leaned closer to her as he said, "Yes, I do need to talk to Cassandra. But I promise we won't yell anymore. Okay?"

Mattie laid her head against the pillow and closed her eyes. JT straightened to his full height and was about to walk away from Mattie when she grabbed his arm. He looked back down at her and saw the tears roll down her face again.

Very slowly, Mattie said, "I . . . was . . . wrong."

JT understood her words as clearly as he understood when

she told him and Cassandra to *stop* a minute ago in the living room. He just wasn't sure if she were saying she was wrong about the lies she'd told on them in the courtroom, the way she'd treated Lily, or the hateful things she'd done and said to him. He wanted to ask for clarification, but then he realized that he didn't need it as he looked at her like a man acquainted with repentance and said, "All is forgiven."

"Thank . . . you," she said in her broken English, and then she turned over and fell asleep.

JT grabbed Cassandra's hand and whispered, "Follow me." He took her upstairs. After opening the door to Jerome and Aaron's room and seeing that Jerome was sound asleep, he walked into their bedroom, closed the door, and then sat Cassandra down on the bed. "Now, please tell me what got you so upset."

"Why do you think I'm upset? You gave our money away," she shouted in his face as she stood up and put her hands on her hips.

"Please lower your voice so we don't wake Jerome or worry your mother any further." He sat down on the bed hoping that would encourage her to sit down also.

"Why'd you give him the money, JT? You knew I didn't want you to do it," she said, still standing.

"I'm just trying to be the kind of man you asked me to be, Sanni. You're not always going to like my decisions, but I need you to trust that I'm just trying to do right by you and the kids."

Cassandra stood in front of him with her hands on her hips. Her neck was twitching as she asked, "What are you talking about, JT?"

Had so much happened since that day he'd come home, when Cassandra decided to trust him, that she'd forgotten what she'd said to him? "Don't you remember, Sanni? When I came home after visiting Lamont in the hospital? We were right in this room when you asked me to be more than just an ordinary man. You wanted me to be God's man."

Recognition flashed in her eyes, but then she turned away from it. "I take it back. I need you to be my man right now." She sat down on the bed next to him and held his hand. "I need you to go downstairs and ask Lamont for that money back. Or at least a hundred thousand of it."

"What's going on, Sanni. Did something happen that I don't know about?"

She lowered her eyes but didn't answer.

JT lifted her chin and asked again, "Is something going on that I don't know about?"

"All right, okay." She stood up and paced the room. "You want to know what's going on? I'll tell you. I had everything resolved. Diane was going to drop her case against you and not try to take custody of Lily. All I had to do was give her a hundred thousand dollars." She lifted her hands, and then let them plop back down against her body. "It's all ruined now. Why'd you have to do it, JT? Why did you give him the money?"

He was sitting there watching his wife speak, but he honestly couldn't believe these words were coming out of her mouth. "Cassandra, do you hear yourself?"

"I know how it sounds. But the ends justify the means. And we could have paid Lamont back eventually."

"Okay, Sanni. Let's say we did it your way. What's to stop Diane from taking that money from us and continuing the lawsuit? It isn't like we could tell the judge that we gave her bribe money, if she refused to hold up her end of the bargain. And believe me, Sanni, that woman would not have held up her end of the bargain."

The look on her face told him that she hadn't considered that Diane could renege on the deal. "Look, Sanni, I know where you're coming from. I've been there." He stood up, put his arms around his wife and continued, "When Sarah died, I stopped trusting God and thought I needed to handle everything myself. But you see where that attitude got us." JT laughed in spite of the situation, and then asked her, "Don't you remember all those self-empowerment messages I used to preach?"

"Nothing gets done unless somebody is doing it," she mimicked the way he used to say that line.

"Yeah, it sounds pretty pathetic to us now. But I had lost my faith in God, so I thought if anything was going to get done, I had to do it myself. I don't believe that anymore, Sanni. I believe God cares about what happens to us and that He is always on the job."

She pounded on his chest and then laid her head on his chest. "I know you're right, but for me, this feels just like losing Sarah all over again. I don't want to lose another child."

"We won't, baby. Trust God. I truly believe He is going to show us a way out of all this drama."

"It's not that easy for me, JT. I need to be sure that things are going to work out for us this time.

"This isn't easy for me either, Sanni. But I've come too far to turn back now. Like it or not, I'm God's man, and I intend to act like it."

Twenty-seven

Cassandra couldn't breathe. She needed to get away. JT wasn't letting her anywhere near their children right now, so she knew she couldn't go far. But she had to get out of the house so she could think. She heard what JT had to say, and she could clearly see that her actions showed that she did not trust God to handle this situation.

She was driving down the street, destination unknown, when she noticed a church building on the right hand side of the street. It wasn't so much the building that she noticed, but the sign in the entrance of the church. It read: *Is it time for your meeting with God? Come on in.* Those words sparked Cassandra's interest because she had tried everything else. She'd been to a therapist, she'd cried, cajoled, and she'd even tried to take money that belonged to someone else, but none of it had solved her problems. So right now, she needed a personal meeting with God like she needed to breathe. She passed the church, but did a u-turn in order to come back around. She parked in the lot and stared at the entrance of the church for a moment. She'd never even noticed this church before, but she was so curious. What type of meeting with God could these people be hosting?

She got out of the car and walked into the building. A scripture that was posted above the sanctuary door read: *For the weapons of our warfare are not carnal, but mighty through God to the pulling down of strongholds.*

Great. Even God knew that she'd been trying to fight her own battles. As far as Cassandra was concerned, that scripture had been posted to the wall the minute she made a u-turn in the street. The entire scripture spoke to her. Yes, she had a stronghold. Cassandra had already called its name: Fear. She had been afraid that JT hadn't truly changed and that he would cheat on her again. That was why she had the panic attacks when he touched her. But when she conquered that fear, it just transferred to her children. Now she was so bound up by the thought of losing them that she could barely function.

She opened the sanctuary door hoping and praying that she would be loosed from her stronghold today. As she walked down the aisle, she noticed that the left side of the sanctuary had been roped off. This big divider was placed behind the ropes so no one could see what was on the other side. The sanctuary was empty. She didn't know what to do or who to ask about her meeting with God, so she sat down on the front pew and waited.

A small man in baggy clothes appeared on the opposite side of the room where the ropes were. Cassandra wondered where he'd come from because she hadn't noticed him before she sat down.

"What are you doing?" he asked her.

Cassandra didn't know this man, and she didn't feel comfortable telling him her business. So she simply said, "Just sitting here."

He looked at her strangely, and then asked, "Don't you think it's rude to keep God waiting?"

"Yes, of course I do," Cassandra answered.

"Then why have you been telling your problems to everyone else, while God has been waiting on you to meet with Him?"

She had no answer for this man. She didn't know him and couldn't understand how he would know that she had been taking her problems everywhere but to God. So she simply said, "Can you please take me to Him?"

"Take off your shoes and follow me," the man said as he released the rope so she could join him on the other side of the sanctuary. She took her pumps off and left them on the floor where she had been sitting. She then walked up the stairs and behind the makeshift wall with the strange man who had also taken his shoes off. Cassandra knew from studying the Old Testament as a child that Mosses was told to take off his shoes because he was on holy ground, just before he spoke with God. Was she truly on holy grounds right now?

The man lead her to a magnificent room with purple drapes, sky blue ceiling, and a floor that was so cushiony it felt as if she were walking on clouds. Beautiful music was playing throughout the room, but it was unlike any music she'd ever heard or could adequately describe. A golden throne was placed in the far corner of the room. She was instructed to kneel down before the throne.

As she knelt down, Cassandra felt as if this overwhelming and consuming presence had stepped into the room. Then she heard a sound and saw multi colored lights flicker around the room. She looked toward the man standing next to her.

He pointed to the throne and said, "Talk to Him."

Her gaze followed his pointer finger to the throne. A man sat there. He was dressed in a white rob, but she could see through the man that was seated on the throne. She turned back to her escort and asked, "Is this some type of trick lighting?"

"Do you want an audience with God or not? Either speak now or continue to carry your burdens on your own."

She thought about getting up and walking out of the room. This man was rude, and she was tired of taking his attitude. But then she realized that he was right. If she left, she'd be leaving with the same burdens she came in with, and she was really tired of carrying them around. So she turned back to the throne and said, "I'm really not sure how to begin. I've always been taught that you have to begin with praise, and then go into your request. But do I praise you when we're in the same room?"

No response.

She got the same non-responsiveness from God when she prayed at home, so why was she here if it weren't going to be any different? But she trudged on anyway. "I'm just going to talk to you. I believe that you care about the things that bother me, but I can't understand why you even allow them in the first place. Like the whole lawsuit from Diane Benson. Why would you allow something like that when JT and I had finally learned to trust one another again?"

She stopped talking for a minute as the word *trust* hung in the air between her and God. She remembered praying to the Lord and hearing the word *trust*. At that time she thought the Lord was trying to get her to trust JT, but had she misunderstood? Yes, she realized, she had totally misunderstood what God tried to tell her that day. She bowed her head as tears sprung to her eyes. "Oh God, forgive me," she cried out as she finally admitted to herself that it had never been as simple as her having a lack of trust in JT. Her panic attacks had not been caused because she feared what JT would do or that she feared losing her children. She'd tried to take that hundred thousand dollars out of their bank account to bribe Diane for one simple reason; she didn't trust God with her life.

In the face of her mistrust of God, she wanted to defend

herself by telling God all that had happened to her in recent years. Who wouldn't have a little mistrust? But deep down she knew that nothing man had done to her should have ever stripped her faith away from God. She had allowed this to occur. And she couldn't blame it on anyone else. JT has asked her to trust God countless times during this ordeal, but she hadn't really heard him. "I want to trust you again, Lord. But if I put my trust in you and things don't turn out right, then what?"

Trust me anyway.

She heard God's answer loud and clear this time, and she wanted . . . no, needed to comply. Life had been too hard when she tried to handle things on her own. "Okay, Lord, help me to trust you and I'll do just that for the rest of my life."

She wiped the tears from her face, stood up, and then turned to thank the man who had brought her into this room. But he was no longer beside her. She turned back to the throne and God had disappeared also. *What was going on in here?* She hurried out of the church, only stopping to put her pumps back on. As she walked out of the building a man in white overalls was taking down the sign that asked, "Is it time for your meeting with God?"

Cassandra ran over to the man and asked him, "Why are you taking that sign down? You all need to keep this going. There are so many other people out there that need to meet with God."

The man looked confused until he read the sign that was in his hand. He turned to Cassandra and said, "I'm sorry, ma'am. The company sent us the wrong sign. It was suppose to be about our annual church meeting. I have to send this one back."

***

JT knocked on the basement door. Lamont opened the door and looked around. "Has she calmed down yet?"

"I don't know if she's calm. But she's gone for a drive."

"She didn't leave you, did she?"

JT shook his head. Lamont was just too inquisitive. "Boy, mind your own business and get out of my way so I can get my kids."

They walked down the stairs, and JT saw that Aaron and Lily were both asleep on the couch. "How long have they been asleep?"

"Pretty much since I brought them down here. I think they were a bit worn out from all the pulling and tugging you and Cassandra were doing with them."

"I'm just glad Jerome hadn't been with her. He's still sleep in his room despite all the commotion." JT sat down in the chair across from the couch and put his head in his hands. He ran his hand through his hair. "I just don't know what got into her."

"I know," Lamont said as he sat down on the arm of the couch. "She didn't want you to give me that money."

When JT didn't respond, Lamont asked, "Why'd you give it to me if you knew she was going to go off the deep end like that?"

"It's your money, Lamont. What else was I suppose to do with it?"

"My dad told me that you kept his money away from him for years and by the time he caught up with you—all the money had been spent. I know you sold your house and car so that you could repay the money, but why didn't you just keep it? You didn't have to come looking for me."

"I had lost my way with God when I took your father's

money. And even though it was money we shouldn't have had in the first place, I had no right to take what didn't belong to me."

"But you could have kept it and nobody would have done anything about it."

"God knew that I owed you. That's who I'm trying to please. I just hate that pleasing God, sometimes means that Cassandra will be unhappy. But that's life," JT said as he stood up and nodded in the direction of his children. "Can you help me take them to their beds?"

JT picked Aaron up while Lamont picked up Lily. They walked up the stairs and put them in their beds. Then JT went to the kitchen and started taking pots and pans out of the cabinet.

"What are you doing?" Lamont asked.

"I'm not sure how long Cassandra will be gone, so I'm going to put something on for dinner so she doesn't have to worry about doing it when she gets home."

Lamont laughed. "You whipped."

"No, I'm married," JT said as he took a pack of ground beef out of the fridge. "And I want to stay that way."

Lamont sat down at the kitchen table. He had a somber expression on his face as he asked, "Look, JT, if you want the money back, just say so? I can't miss what I never had."

JT opened the cabinet and took down a box of spaghetti and then started putting water in a pot. As he sat the pot of water on the stove and turned it on, he turned back to Lamont. "Do you suppose that God would tell me to give that money to you just so I could ask for it back?"

Lamont put his elbow on the table, his hand under his chin, and leaned on the table as he pondered the question for a moment. He then said, "I don't suppose so."

"Then I don't want your money back."

Lamont played like he was wiping the sweat from his brow. "Good. Because that Escalade was calling my name."

JT threw the oven mitt at Lamont. "That Escalade is too expensive for you, boy. You need to be able to pay your bills while you're in school, or are you even thinking that far ahead?"

"Put your spaghetti in the pot; I got this. I know what I'm doing. Me and my lady are going to look good riding down the street in something like that."

JT opened the box of spaghetti, broke the noodles in half and threw them in the boiling water. He opened the pack of ground beef, put it in the skillet and started pulling it apart with a fork. "Okay, you think you know what you're doing. But do one thing for me, pray and ask God which car He thinks you should have at this point in your life."

Before Lamont could respond, the front door opened and Cassandra walked in. She peeked around the corner, saw Lamont sitting at the table and headed for the kitchen.

Lamont stood up. He looked like he'd just been caught swiping the last cookie or something. "I'm going to head on back downstairs. I'll talk to you later, JT."

"Wait, don't leave," Cassandra said as she entered the kitchen.

Lamont waved her off as he backed away from the table. "I'm just trying to stay out the way. I'll be looking for my own place as soon as I get some wheels."

She put her hand on the chair Lamont had just exited. "Please, sit back down. I owe you an apology."

JT was standing at the stove. He had a spatula in his hand, turning over the hamburger. He recognized the change in his wife the moment she walked into the kitchen. He didn't know where she went when she left the house, but he knew one thing for sure, Cassandra had been with God . . . and she'd found peace.

As Lamont sat back down, Cassandra turned to JT with a smile of appreciation. "You're cooking."

"Somebody had to feed this family," he joked as he light-heartedly picked the dish rag out of the sink and threw it at her. When she caught it, he said, "You've got dishes."

"Gladly," she said with just as big a smile on her face as JT wore on his.

Not able to stand it any longer, JT walked over to his wife and hugged her. She felt good in his arms. He was so glad he had made it home before she took the kids and left. "I'm glad you came back so soon."

"I am too," she said, returning the hug. "But I owe you guys an apology, and I need to handle that right now." Cassandra sat down.

JT quickly went back over to the stove, poured the spa-ghetti in a strainer and turned off the fire under the spaghetti and ground beef pots. He sat down next to his wife and held her hand.

Cassandra looked directly at Lamont and began. "I went to the bank this morning to take a hundred thousand out of our account. I was going to give it to Lily's mom so she'd drop this case against JT and agree not to try and take Lily away from us.

"Earlier today, I wanted to leave JT. I felt like he was ruin-ing all of our lives by not giving that money to Diane. But when I left here without my children, I was just driving aim-lessly. Then I went to this church and had a meeting with God."

"You had what?" Lamont asked with a raised brow.

"Yeah." Cassandra smiled, as she continued, "The church had a special room set up with a throne and everything. But when I left the church, I found out that the sign had been a mistake, so I'm still trying to figure that one out.

"Anyway, once I had my meeting with God, I realized that fear had become a stronghold in my life because I stopped trusting God. But I am claiming the victory today. And I want both of you to know that I am so sorry for the way I acted."

Squeezing his wife's hand, JT asked, "So are you with me on this now, Sanni?"

She poked JT in the side as she lightheartedly said, "You have frustrated me throughout this whole ordeal. So I've decided to be with God on this one."

"That's good enough for me, baby," JT said with a smile. "If you're with God, then you're definitely with me also."

Twenty-eight

Judge Landon took his seat. The bailiff instructed everyone to be seated, and as Cassandra took her seat behind JT, she determined that no matter what happened today, she would not freak out. It had been a month since she'd had her personal meeting with God, and Cassandra had prayed ever since that day for the strength to get through these court proceedings without having a panic attack.

JT turned to her and asked, "Are you sure you want to sit in here today?"

A couple weeks ago they had found out that although Margie had withdrawn her name from the lawsuit, she had been subpoenaed. So JT was worried that Cassandra was going to spaz out when she heard Margie's testimony. But it wasn't Margie's words that sent Cassandra reeling, it was Bishop Turner's.

Margie stepped down from the witness chair looking like this was the last place she wanted to be. Cassandra understood her; this was the last place she wanted to be also. She hoped with all that was in her that no more women would decide to sue her husband. She'd have to kill him if they did.

As Margie walked past her, Cassandra noted the brokenness of the woman and knew that JT was responsible for her current condition. She wanted to put her arm around the woman and comfort her. But how does one comfort the ex-lover of their husband? Margie stopped. Cassandra tensed as she watched Margie turn in her direction. *Please God, don't let her say something foul to me. I was having sympathy for her. So I really don't want to beat her down in this courthouse.*

Margie looked at Cassandra and whispered through teary eyes, "I'm sorry."

Unable to speak because of the knot forming in her throat, Cassandra simply nodded. Before she could recover from the emotions she felt at accepting Margie's apology, Bishop Turner was called to the stand. Cassandra rolled her eyes, preparing herself for the lies that were sure to come out of her secret father's mouth.

"Do you swear to tell the whole truth..." The bailiff said his normal lines as each new witness was put on the stand.

Bishop promised to tell the truth, and Cassandra scoffed. "He wouldn't know the truth if it fell on his head," she whispered in JT's ear.

Luke stood to begin his examination. He looked over some papers on his table, winked at Diane, and then turned toward Bishop. "Now, Bishop Turner, if my records are correct, you've been the overseer of Faith Outreach and about nine other churches for about thirty-seven years. Is that correct?"

"Yes, I was a pastor for five years. Then when my father passed away, I took over his responsibilities as bishop."

"In your thirty-seven years as bishop of numerous churches, I'm sure you've dealt with a lot of issues."

Bishop seemed to squirm in his seat as he adjusted his tie. "It's part of the job."

Luke smiled as if he were having a conversation with an old friend. "Is it part of the job to clean up after these pastors who can't seem to keep their pants up?"

Bishop coughed and sputtered as if he'd just swallowed something that went down the wrong way.

"I'm sorry, Bishop. Do you need a drink of water?" Luke asked as he walked over to his table and poured water from the ice cold pitcher on his table into a glass. He walked back over to Bishop Turner and handed it to him.

Bishop Turner drank the water as if he had just been rescued from a desert island and was dying of thirst.

"Now, can you answer the question for me, sir? How many pastors within your fellowship have had affairs with members of their congregation?"

With a look of indignation, Bishop asked, "How am I supposed to know that?"

Luke took the glass out of Bishop Turner's hand and put it on the defense table. He then walked back to bishop and said, "Isn't it your job to know what's going on with the pastors in your fellowship?" Without waiting for an answer he said, "Okay then, let me rephrase the question. Are you aware of any incidents within your fellowship of churches where a pastor was caught having an affair with a member of his church?"

"There have been a few," Bishop admitted.

"And of these few, how many times have you had this issue with Pastor Thomas?"

Bishop was non-responsive as he sat in his seat staring down at his shoes.

Luke turned to Judge Landon. "Will you please instruct the witness to answer the question?"

Judge Landon swiveled in his chair so that he faced Bishop Turner and said, "Answer the question."

Bishop lifted his head. He turned toward JT and held his gaze for a moment. His eyes filled with sympathy and compassion.

JT nodded, as if to say, *It's okay, answer the question.*

Bishop turned from JT and admitted, "Three times."

"Three times!" Luke said the words as if he'd just heard a shocking development. He then turned around to face the onlookers in the courtroom and said again, "Three times!" He strutted around, shaking his head in disgust, then turned back to Bishop and asked, "Would you say that is a bit excessive for a man of God to be caught in *three* separate affairs?"

"Yes," Bishop mumbled, the words barely audible.

Luke put his hand to his ear. "What? I didn't hear your response."

"I said, yes." Bishop was louder this time.

"And your job is to protect these pastors when they get caught in indiscretions, right?"

"I wouldn't say that."

"Then what would you say? Because you sure didn't protect Margie, or Vivian Sampson, or my client." He turned and pointed at Diane. She clung to Joe as if she had been so traumatized by all of this, that she couldn't even hold herself upright without help.

"In fact, Bishop, when Margie told you what was going on, you told her it was best that she transfer her membership to another church, didn't you?"

"Th . . .that's n . . . not true. I tried to help Margie. I thought it would be best if she went to another church, so that she didn't have to continue seeing JT. But it wasn't how you're trying to make it seem."

"Really?" Luke said with an I-got-you-now expression on his face. "Well then, when Diane Benson called and told you that she'd just had a baby by Pastor Thomas, can you tell the court just how you helped her?"

Bishop found something else of interest on his shoes.

"Answer the question please," Judge Landon interjected.

When Bishop still didn't respond, Luke said, "Didn't you,

in fact, tell my client to keep quiet and just let her poor husband continue to think that the child was his?"

Gasps were heard across the courtroom as the onlookers listened to the unthinkable.

"Aren't men of God supposed to repent when they've done something wrong? But if they have you playing God on earth, covering up their actions, why do they need to repent to the God in heaven?"

"I've never tried to play God. And in normal circumstances, I wouldn't have tried to cover that up either."

"Ah, but why wouldn't Pastor Thomas have been treated like any other pastor within your fellowship?" Luke paused as Bishop squirmed. He then turned and spotted Cassandra and pointed at her. "It's because of her, isn't it, Bishop?"

Cassandra saw the look of horror on Bishop's face. She had no idea how Diane's attorney found out that she was Bishop Turner's daughter, but she knew where he was going with this line of questioning. And she couldn't let him do it. Yes, she wanted her father to admit that she belonged to him, but not like this... not being forced like this. She stood up, and for the second time in a month, interrupted another judge's courtroom. "Stop! Leave him alone!" she screamed.

"Sit down, baby girl. It's high time that I atone for my sins," Bishop said as tears flowed down his cheeks.

"Don't do it. You don't have to," she told him. She didn't want to be responsible for him losing everything, which is surely what would happen if he admitted in open court that she was his daughter."

Bishop sat up straighter in his seat, wiped the tears from his face and said, "You are right. Cassandra was the reason this situation was different. She's my daughter, and I didn't want her hurt by what JT had done."

"Don't you mean, your illegitimate daughter?"

Gasps went around the courtroom again. Several reporters jumped up and quickly left the room, having received their scoop for the day.

"How long have you been married, Bishop?"

"Forty-two years," he announced proudly.

"And how old is your *illegitimate* daughter?" Luke asked.

"She's thirty-six." He ran his hand from his forehead to the back of his neck. "Look, I'm not proud of what I did. Yes, you're right. I had a daughter by another woman, but my wife and I love Cassandra. I'm just sorry it took me this long to publicly acknowledge that she's mine. Because it has been a blessing to my soul everyday she has been alive." He turned to Cassandra, and without caring about hidden secrets or the consequences that were sure to come, he said, "I love you, baby girl. That's a fact." He then lowered his head and his shoulders shook as his heart released years of unshed tears.

Watching her father breakdown like that was heart wrenching for Cassandra. She had worshipped this man for so long, adored him and sought only to please him. But that had been when she thought he was her godfather. Once she found out that he was her father, she'd been struggling to forgive him for all the years of denial and deception. But seeing just how much his own deception had hurt him also, broke something in Cassandra and she found that she no longer had the strength to hold a grudge against her father. She wanted him back in her life... needed him.

Luke appeared shaken by the apparent broken man before him. He stepped back and told the judge. "I have no further questions."

Judge Landon brought the gavel down. "We will adjourn this case until tomorrow."

Cassandra stood up and ran to Bishop. The bailiff held out his hand, stopping her from entering the witness box. Bishop stood and came to her. They hugged and cried in one another's arms. Just as they were breaking apart, Cassandra whispered, "I love you too, Daddy."

Twenty-nine

"I hate to break it to you, but you're getting your hats handed to you in that courtroom. Now I see why Mrs. T wanted that money," Lamont said as he sat at the kitchen table with JT and Bishop.

"She hasn't won yet. There's a whole other side that the judge hasn't heard yet. Just wait, our turn is coming," JT said confidently.

"You say that like you've got a trick up your sleeve," Bishop said.

JT looked back and saw Cassandra sitting with her mother in the family room. He turned back to Bishop and said, "I do, but I don't want to say anything right now. I don't want Cassandra to overhear, and then get excited, just in case things don't go the way I expect them to."

"All right, son," Bishop said as he patted JT on the shoulder and stood. "I'll see you tomorrow in court, but right now I need to go talk to Mattie."

JT stood up. "Are you sure you want to do that? I mean, yeah, she's been a lot easier to deal with since the stroke, but I'm not sure if she's mellowed any toward you."

"I'm tired of hiding from it, JT. I owe Mattie an apology that's thirty-six years late in coming," Bishop said, and then left JT and Lamont in the kitchen as he went into the family room.

JT turned to Lamont and said, "I need you to be on time tomorrow."

"I got this," Lamont said while slapping his chest. "Don't worry about a thing."

JT then turned toward the family room and watched Bishop say something to Cassandra. Cassandra then left the room and came into the kitchen with him.

"What's going on?" she asked, JT.

JT couldn't take his eyes off Mattie and Bishop Turner. "He said he's going to apologize."

"What? I've got to see this." Cassandra turned toward the family room and invaded her parents' privacy.

"What's the big deal? I apologize to people all the time," Lamont said.

"Yeah, but you never got on Mattie Daniels's bad side," JT said.

They were all gawking into the family room now. They each watched in amazement as Mattie sat up and stretched out her hand to Bishop. He shook it and a truce between the two of them, although almost forty years late, had finally been forged.

JT turned to Cassandra and said, "Did you see that?"

"I see it. I just don't believe what I'm seeing," she replied.

"Just think, Sanni. If God can bring a truce between those two, imagine what He can do for us."

The next day in the courtroom, JT and Cassandra witnessed a bit of what God could do for them. Their attorney, Tom quickly cross-examined Bishop Turner, and then let him get off the stand without any more damage to his reputation.

Then Diane took the stand, she raised her right hand and

affirmed to tell the truth. She then sat down, and the judge, her lawyer, and anyone else listening heard that she and her husband had a happy marriage before JT seduced her.

When it was Tom's turn to cross-examine her, he reviewed his notes as if he hadn't already read the information numerous times. He then turned to Diane and said, "Now, Mrs. Benson, you stated that if it hadn't been for JT, you and your husband would have a perfect marriage. Is that correct?"

"Well, yes. I love my husband and would never have cheated on him if JT hadn't manipulated me into the whole affair," Diane said in her poor-me-I'm-an-innocent-pawn voice.

"You also stated that JT is the only man you've ever cheated on your husband with. Is that correct?"

"Didn't I already say that?" Diane was becoming defiant now.

Tom turned his back to Diane and faced the outer court as he said, "Mr. Johnson, would you please stand up?"

Brian Johnson stood up and waved at Diane.

Tom turned back to his witness and asked, "Do you recognize Mr. Johnson?"

Diane glared at Tom.

"Can you answer the question, Mrs. Benson? And please remember that you swore to tell the truth."

"Of course I know Brian. He used to work for my husband."

"When you left your husband last year, didn't you leave with Mr. Johnson?" Tom asked.

"Objection!" Luke said as he jumped from his seat. "Your, honor, he's trying to villainize the victim."

"The witness opened the door when she claimed that she had only cheated on her husband with Mr. Thomas. I should therefore, be allowed to cross on her sworn testimony."

"Overruled, the witness may answer," Judge Landon declared.

Diane rolled her eyes as she said, "I most certainly did not leave town with the likes of Brian Johnson." Diane's voice elevated to the point where it was obvious to everyone that she was irritated by the line of questioning.

Tom walked back to his table, opened a file folder, pulled out a document and walked back over to Diane. He held the document in front of her. "What is this document?"

Diane reviewed the document and then answered, "It's a lease agreement."

"And can you tell us the names of the tenants on the lease agreement?" Tom asked.

Rolling her eyes again, she leaned back in her seat and said, "Diane Benson and Brian Johnson."

Oohs and aahs could be heard throughout the courtroom. Judge Landon banged his gavel. "Quiet in the courtroom."

Tom then asked, "If you didn't leave town with Mr. Johnson, how did your names get on the rental agreement just four days after you left Cleveland?"

Her eyes were focused on the ceiling. With tight lips she said, "I don't know."

Benson stood up and yelled at Diane. "What do you mean you don't know? You told me you left town to think. You swore to me that you hadn't left with Brian."

Luke stood up and grabbed Benson's arm. He leaned over and whispered in his ear. "Sit down, man. You can't do this in court."

Benson yanked his arm out of Luke's grasp, and then sat back down.

"What about Darryl Mills?" Tom asked when things quieted back down.

"What about him?" Diane asked defiantly.

"Did you start having an affair with the very married Mr. Darryl Mills after Mr. Johnson left you in Jacksonville, Florida?"

"Is there a point to this line of questioning?" Luke said, back on his feet again.

Judge Landon squared his eyes on Tom and said, "The counselor does have a point. I don't know how many more men I'm going to allow you to bring up in the courtroom today. It is beginning to appear as if you're trying to make Mrs. Benson the villain."

"No, sir," Tom hurriedly said. "I don't believe that Mrs. Benson is a villain, but I don't think she's a victim either. She and JT were both two adults who willingly decided to do something they knew was wrong. And furthermore, Mrs. Benson hasn't stopped, so how traumatized could she be from her affair with Mr. Thomas?"

In true dramatic form, Luke stood back up, threw his pen across the table and bellowed, "Objection! Your Honor, how much more of this does my client have to endure?"

Tom looked toward the door, hoping that it would swing open and the person he was waiting on would run into the courtroom. When the door didn't open, he turned to Judge Landon and said, "Your Honor, I do have one more thing to ask the witness, but I need a ten minute recess before I can continue."

It was ten o'clock, and Lamont was no where near the courthouse. He had stopped at a copy center so he could download the pictures from his camera and print them out. Once he paid for his computer usage and the printing, he jumped back in the 2007 Buick LaCrosse that JT talked him into buying. He needed to be at the courthouse in twenty minutes so that he could give the photos he'd taken to Tom Albright, but the car wouldn't start.

He popped the hood, got out the car, and slammed the door. "See what being cheap does? I bet that Escalade would have started right up."

Lamont didn't have much experience under the hood of a car, so he tinkered with a few of the plugs and then closed the hood. He got back in the car and tried to start it again, but didn't turn over. He tapped his fingers on the dashboard as he tried to figure out what might be wrong with the car. The battery . . . it's the battery, he thought as he got back out the car. He looked around wondering where he would find some cables to jump his battery.

"Are you waiting on a witness?" Judge Landon asked while looking at the notes in front of him. "You don't have another witness logged for today."

"No, Your Honor," Tom said. "I don't have another witness for today. I need to present the court with evidence for my next line of questioning."

"Objection," Luke said. "I wasn't informed about any evidence that council wants to present to the court."

"I was just made aware of this evidence last night," Tom informed Judge Landon.

Judge Landon looked at Tom as if he were getting ready to deny his request.

Tom raised his hand and said, "Your Honor, here is the bottom line. I believe this case needs to be dismissed because of collusion."

"What are you talking about, Mr. Albright?" Judge Landon asked with a scowl on his face.

Tom took a deep breath and plowed ahead. "I believe that the defendant and her attorney have cooked up this case for the sole purpose of extorting money from my client's former church." He pointed at Diane as she sat in the witness chair looking like a tiger, ready to pounce on her prey. "Because if the court believes that this woman was manipulated into have sex with my client, then it would stand to reason that Mr. Watson also manipulated her, since he is a man of authority as well."

Judge Landon leaned his elbows on his desktop and fixed Tom with a look that had caused a multitude of men to confess to their misdeeds. "Are you accusing Mr. Watson of sleeping with his client?"

"Thanks, man, I appreciate your help," Lamont said to the guy who had just jump started his car. He got back in his car and raced to the courthouse. JT had done so much for him. He just wanted to help JT out in his time of need. And he had found a way. Lamont had googled Diane Benson and found her address. He staked out the house for several nights, following her whenever she left the house.

A few nights ago he hit pay dirt. Diane met a man in a hotel room and Lamont was there to photograph it.

"I can prove it, Your Honor. I just need a few more minutes." Tom looked toward the door with a longing expression on his face. *Come on, Lamont.*

As if he'd heard Tom's plea, the door to the courtroom

opened, and Lamont walked in with a manila envelope in his hand. He looked at Tom and nodded.

Tom stepped away from the bench and signaled Lamont to approach. Lamont handed him the manila envelope, and then sat down and wiped the sweat from his forehead. Tom turned back to the judge and said, "Mr. Lamont Stevens informed my client of these pictures yesterday. I viewed them on his camera, but asked that he print them out so that I might present them to the court." Tom handed the photos to Judge Landon. "As you can see, Your Honor, the photos clearly show Mr. Watson and Mrs. Benson in bed together."

The courtroom erupted. Benson stood up and punched Luke in the face. "How dare you take my money and sleep with my wife too."

"Joe, it's not true," Diane yelled from the witness stand.

"I don't want to hear another word from you. I'm done," he told her as he grabbed hold of Luke's shirt and hauled off and punched him again.

Luke fell to the ground and quickly crawled away from Benson. "They're lying. I didn't sleep with your wife."

"I want my money back," Benson said as two bailiffs grabbed him and hauled him out of the courtroom.

Judge Landon tried to regain order. He banged on the gavel several times. Once the noise had subsided, Judge Landon told Luke to get off the floor. When Luke stood up, Judge Landon held the pictures out to him and asked, "Can you explain this?"

Luke wiped the blood away from his lip with some tissue and then grabbed the pictures. He began sputtering, but no real words escaped his mouth.

"You shouldn't be her attorney in this case, and you know it. I'm granting the defendants' motion and dismissing this case." Judge Landon brought the gavel down one final time, and then stood. But before stepping down from the bench he told Luke, "I want to see you in my chambers at nine in the morning."

Cassandra jumped up, put her arms around JT's neck, and pulled him close to her. "You did it! You did it!"

JT whispered in her ear, "I told you we didn't need Lamont's money."

"No, just his camera," Cassandra said as she turned to find Lamont. When she spotted him she mouthed, "Thank you."

Her spirits were lifted until she watched Diane storm her way over to them. With one hand on her hip and the other pointing in JT's face she said, "It's not over. Oh, I promise you that."

JT lifted his hands. "Look, Diane, I'm tired of fighting. You, me, and Cassandra may never see eye to eye on everything, but I'm hoping that we can agree to parent together."

With the sista-sista neck going, Diane said, "How are we going to parent together when you're trying to take my parental rights away?" She pointed at her chest. "I birthed Lily, JT. Me, not Cassandra."

He squeezed Cassandra's hand as he said, "We realize that, Diane. And I'm willing to work out visitation rights with you."

Cassandra looked at JT as if he'd lost his mind.

He simply patted her hand and said, "It's the right thing to do . . . for Lily."

Cassandra nodded. She knew he was right. If they kept Lily away from Diane, she would always blame them for her lack of a relationship with her birth mother. Better to let Lily figure out for herself whether or not she wanted Diane in her life.

Diane looked toward the door where Benson had been escorted out of after he punched Luke. "It might take awhile before I can visit with her. I think I'm going to be looking for a place to stay." As she walked away, sadness clung to her eyes.

JT turned to Tom, shook his hand, and thanked him for everything.

"You did the work, man." Tom laughed, and then said, "I can't believe it; Luke and Diane handed us such a gift. I thought we were going to lose."

"See. That just shows that you ought to trust God more." JT patted Tom on the back, and then walked out of the courtroom hand in hand with his wife.

When they got in JT's car, Cassandra leaned over and hugged him. "You're a good man, JT Thomas."

"Those words sound a lot like forgiveness to me, Mrs. Thomas."

She kissed him, then said, "With the help of God, I have learned to trust you again, so yes, I can now say that I truly forgive you for everything you put me through." Then she held up a warning finger and added, "But don't let it happen again."

"Woman, you didn't marry no fool. I've got my good thang, and I'm not trying to lose you ever again."

He started the car, and as they drove down the street, Yolanda Adams's song, "I Got the Victory" came on the radio. Cassandra thought the song was fitting because they had definitely been through the storm and the rain. And just like the song said, Cassandra truly knew all about heartache and pain, but God had brought her through it all. "Blessed be the name of the Lord," Cassandra said as she turned up the volume, leaned back in her seat, and enjoyed the drive home.

Reader's Discussion Questions

1. JT had been a cheater, but God forgave him, and from that point, he desired to do what was right. But Cassandra struggled to forgive her husband. Do you think you could stay married to a man like JT Thomas?

2. JT's high school Sweetheart (Erica) had prayed for his salvation and deliverance for years without ever knowing if her prayers had been answered, even though JT had broken her heart. Could you pray for someone who had hurt you?

3. Cassandra's lack of trust in God caused her to struggle with panic attacks and unforgiveness. Has anything ever happened in your life that caused you to lose trust in God?

4. At one point in the story, JT considered himself to be a victim of his own adulterous affair. However, Cassandra didn't agree with him. What do you think? Who are the real victims when a pastor sins? Could it be his wife, the children, and the church members? Who else?

5. Mattie was very bitter and unforgiving. Her bitterness eventually affected her health. What about you? Are there things you need to let go of? Do you believe harboring bitterness can affect your health?

6. Bishop Turner suffered for years because of his hidden secrets. What do you think? Should Bishop Turner have admitted that Cassandra was his daughter when she was first

born? Or do you believe he was right to hide his sins from the church?

7. Which minor character would you like to know more about: Diane Benson, Margie Milner or Lamont Stevens? E-mail me at <u>vmiller-01@earthlink.net</u> and let me know.

About the Author

Vanessa Miller of Dayton, Ohio is an Essence bestselling author, playwright, and motivational speaker. Her stage productions include: **"Get You Some Business", "Don't Turn Your Back on God", "Can't You Hear Them Crying", and "Abundant Rain". Vanessa is currently in the process of turning all the novels in the Rain Series into stage productions.**

Vanessa has been writing since she was a young child. When she wasn't writing poetry, short stories, stage plays, and novels, reading consumed her free time. However, it wasn't until she committed her life to the Lord in 1994 that she realized all gifts and anointings come from God. She then set out to write redemption stories that glorified God.

To date, Vanessa has written the Rain Series and the Storm Series. The books in the Rain Series are: *Former Rain, Abundant Rain,* and *Latter Rain.* The books in the Storm Series are: *Rain Storm* and *Through The Storm.* These books have received rave reviews, winning Best Christian Fiction Awards and topping numerous bestsellers lists. Vanessa believes that each book in The Rain and Storm Series will touch readers across the country in a special way. It is, after all, her God-given destiny to write and produce plays and novels that bring deliverance to God's people.

Vanessa self-published her first three books, then in 2006

she signed a five-book deal with Urban Christian/Urban Books, LLC, distributed by Kensington Corp. Her books can now be found in Wal-Mart, most all major bookstores, including African American bookstores and online bookstores such as Amazon.com.

Vanessa is a dedicated Christian and devoted mother. She graduated from Capital University with a degree in Organizational Communication. In 2007 Vanessa was ordained by her church as an exhorter, which of course, Vanessa believes was the right position for her because God has called her to exhort readers and to help them rediscover their place with the Lord.

A perfect day for Vanessa is one that affords her the time to curl up with a good book. Vanessa has just completed the Forsaken Series and is currently working on other novels. Go to: www.vanessamiller.com for more info on Vanessa and her books.

ORDER FORM
URBAN BOOKS, LLC
78 E. Industry Ct
Deer Park, NY 11729

Name:(please print):_____

Address: _____

City/State: _____

Zip: _____

QTY	TITLES	PRICE
	A Man's Worth	$14.95
	Abundant Rain	$14.95
	Battle Of Jericho	$14.95
	By The Grace Of God	$14.95
	Dance Into Destiny	$14.95
	Divorcing The Devil	$14.95
	Forsaken	$14.95
	Grace And Mercy	$14.95
	Guilty & Not Guilty Of Love	$14.95
	His Woman, His Wife His Widow	$14.95
	Illusion	$14.95
	The LoveChild	$14.95

Shipping and Handling - add $3.50 for 1st book then $1.75 for each additional book.
Please send a check payable to:
   Urban Books, LLC
Please allow 4 - 6 weeks for delivery

ORDER FORM
URBAN BOOKS, LLC
78 E. Industry Ct
Deer Park, NY 11729

Name: (please print): _____

Address: _____

City/State: _____

Zip: _____

QTY	TITLES	PRICE
	The Cartel	$14.95
	The Cartel#2	$14.95
	The Dopeman's Wife	$14.95
	The Prada Plan	$14.95
	Gunz And Roses	$14.95
	Snow White	$14.95
	A Pimp's Life	$14.95
	Hush	$14.95
	Little Black Girl Lost 1	$14.95
	Little Black Girl Lost 2	$14.95
	Little Black Girl Lost 3	$14.95
	Little Black Girl Lost 4	$14.95

Shipping and Handling - add $3.50 for 1st book then $1.75 for each additional book.
Please send a check payable to:
Urban Books, LLC
Please allow 4 - 6 weeks for delivery

ORDER FORM
URBAN BOOKS, LLC
78 E. Industry Ct
Deer Park, NY 11729

Name: (please print): _____

Address: _____

City/State: _____

Zip: _____

QTY	TITLES	PRICE
	16 ½ On The Block	$14.95
	16 On The Block	$14.95
	Betrayal	$14.95
	Both Sides Of The Fence	$14.95
	Cheesecake And Teardrops	$14.95
	Denim Diaries	$14.95
	Happily Ever Now	$14.95
	Hell Has No Fury	$14.95
	If It Isn't love	$14.95
	Last Breath	$14.95
	Loving Dasia	$14.95
	Say It Ain't So	$14.95

Shipping and Handling - add $3.50 for 1st book then $1.75 for each additional book.
Please send a check payable to:
Urban Books, LLC
Please allow 4 - 6 weeks for delivery

ORDER FORM
URBAN BOOKS, LLC
78 E. Industry Ct
Deer Park, NY 11729

Name: (please print):_____

Address: _____

City/State: _____

Zip: _____

QTY	TITLES	PRICE

Shipping and Handling - add $3.50 for 1st book then $1.75 for each additional book.

Please send a check payable to:

Urban Books, LLC

Please allow 4 - 6 weeks for delivery

Notes

Notes